LET IT BE MORNING

SAYED KASHUA

Translated from the Hebrew
by
Miriam Shlesinger

Atlantic Books
London

First published in the United States of America in 2006 by Black Cat,
a paperback original imprint of Grove/Atlantic Inc.

First published as a paperback original in Great Britain in 2007
by Atlantic Books, an imprint of Grove Atlantic Ltd.

3 5 7 9 8 6 4 2

A CIP catalogue record for this book is available from the British Library.

ISBN: 978 1 84354 543 9

Printed and bound in Great Britain by Bookmarque Ltd, Croydon

Atlantic Books
An imprint of Grove Atlantic Ltd
Ormond House
26–27 Boswell Street
London WC1N 3JZ

LET IT BE
MORNING

Sayed Kashua was born in 1975 in Galilee and studied
at the Hebrew University in Jerusalem. He writes a
weekly column for *Ha'aretz*, Israel's most prestigious
newspaper, and lives with his wife and two children in
Beit-Safafa, an Arab village within Jerusalem. His first
novel, *Dancing Arabs*, was a San Francisco Book of the
Year and was translated into eight languages.

To Najaat and Nai

LET IT BE
MORNING

PART ONE

*Everything Has to Be
Wonderful Here*

1

The door gives a terrible screech as my mother opens it. The children's bedroom gives off a musty smell, like a secondhand bookstore that people hardly visit. She hurries over to the window and opens it, wipes some of the dust off the desk with her dust cloth, and says "See, nothing's changed." And I look at her, so changed, so tired, so old. She gives me her usual look, the one that always says everything will be okay.

"The food will be ready in a minute."

"I'm not hungry, Mom."

"I bet you haven't eaten since this morning. Come on, eat it while it's still warm. It'll take a while. Go take a nap, and I'll call you. There's pea soup too."

My mother is sensitive enough to close the door on her way out. I look around the room I left ten years ago. Nothing's changed, except for the fact that nobody lives in it. The three cots stand empty, evenly spaced. I was the first of the three brothers to leave this room, and now I'm the first to return. Nothing's changed, except perhaps the smell, which I still can't manage to ignore, and now I can imagine what being forsaken smells like.

I put down my duffel bag, the black one that's been with me ever since my university days, and lie down on the middle bed, the one that was always mine. The feel of the bed is further evidence that nobody has visited this room in a good many years. The mattress gives off a kind of dampness, and by the smell of the sheets and the pillow I can tell that my mother hasn't changed them since we left for the last time. I look up at the high ceiling and see some green and black circles of mildew on the section right above me. Once my father would fix the leaks right away, climbing up on the roof and applying special sealants, then painting over them. Judging by the big stain, he doesn't bother anymore, as if the children's room isn't part of the house now. As if it doesn't really exist.

I never imagined this room could be so quiet. This room, which once buzzed with life, with screaming and games and countless squabbles, is utterly still now, everything frozen in place, everything just so. The books on the shelves have been arranged in order of the grades in which we used them. My mother hasn't thrown out so much as a single book, not even the ones from elementary school. They're all there in the bookcase. And our three names are still written on the three drawers, as if we're still liable to fight over who gets which one. Three chairs, side by side, evenly spaced, face the long desk that Father made especially for us. He forced us to do all our homework there, sitting stiffly on our chairs, which we weren't allowed to move an inch. My father took exact measurements, and drew four circles on the floor for each of the chairs. That's where the legs had to stay. As we grew taller, he would move the circles, seeing to it that the distance from the desk fit our new size. Nothing pleased him more than to come home, open the boys' room and see us sitting in our set positions, our faces immersed in books and notebooks. We always made a point of assuming that favorite pose of his when we knew he was about to return from work. It was no trouble. In fact, it was kind of fun, and as soon as he shut the door behind him, no matter how much we'd been fighting, we'd almost always give each other the look, and giggle.

My chair was in the middle, the one farthest from the desk. I get up off the bed and look at it. I was the largest one in the family, taller even than my older brother. I take a good look at the floor and discover that the red marks are still there, and that the chairs are positioned right on the last circles Father etched into it. I take my seat, the middle one, and discover that my body hasn't grown since I finished high school. The chair is exactly the right distance from the desk, and my posture is just right, almost completely straight. And as I try to pretend to be writing, my body leans forward in the chair at precisely the angle that Father claimed was the healthiest and the best one. I smile now, and the smile gives me a strange feeling, like when a muscle that's been slack for a long time wakes up, coming back into use.

I reach out to the drawer that bears my name in thick red letters and pull it out till it nearly touches my stomach. The drawer is filled with papers, meticulously arranged, all the way to the top, till there isn't room for even one more sheet. I pull out the whole stack and put it on the desk in front of me. My mother has kept everything in order. Even the picture they gave us when we finished kindergarten is in that drawer. A blue sky, a yellow sun with eyes and a smiling mouth, and red flowers. It's all there, sorted by year, in sequence, every report card from first to twelfth grade, trimester by trimester. Class pictures of every single year. Right on top is my matriculation certificate, and below it the high school class picture. Every kid in my class, in little squares, row by row along the bottom half. Above them are the passport pictures of my teachers, in bigger squares. And in the top center is the principal, who got the biggest picture of all, right above the school name and logo.

The students' pictures are so small you can hardly make out their faces. If it weren't for the names underneath each one, in tiny letters too, I'd never find my own. I take a close look at the little square that contains me and remember how scared I was of leaving this room, this place. How I'd been 100 percent certain that this was where I wanted to stay forever. How I'd spent the whole night crying before moving to a different city, to study there and live there. And how the place that had always been home to me gradually began to seem menacing. I remember how on the day I left, carrying my black duffel bag, the only thing I wanted was for my three years of school to go by quickly so I could hurry back. How I'd sobbed when all the neighbors and all our relatives, who make a habit of coming to say good-bye during the week before someone leaves, kept congregating in our yard each evening, bringing presents, comforting my parents and trying to cheer them up. How I'd cried when I left, how I was crying now, when I had no choice but to return.

I look at the little square photos beside mine. I used to think I'd never forget my schoolmates, and now, as I look them over, I discover that I haven't thought back about a single one of them. The kids in my class always seemed to me like a blob of faces following me wherever I went, but as I look at this class picture and study them one by one, they seem so odd, so distant. Even their names have been blotted out of my memory in the ten years that have gone by. I haven't spoken with any of them in all that time, or before that either, but at least I used to see them almost every day. Why the hell do I imagine them now as more dangerous than they were? Why am I afraid of them, afraid of bumping into them?

I read the names out loud, and they grab me and take me back. God, who are all these people? What are they doing now? And I go on studying their pictures: Jamil Hazkhiyyeh, Nabil Nasser, Haytham Sultan, Hanan Fadilla. I've forgotten them all, the students, the teachers, the principal. But I'm back now, and I'll have no choice. They're nearby, practically next door, and I'm bound to bump into them. I've got to be careful. I stare at the papers, one by one, and read the comments the teachers wrote over the years. I didn't receive a single bad mark, except in subjects like phys ed and shop and metalworking. I thumb through the pages in awe, turning them carefully and placing them one on top of the other, taking care not to do anything that would upset the order my mother had imposed.

2

I wake to the sounds of the TV. My parents continue to be early risers, even though neither one of them works anymore. I'll stay in bed a little longer. I haven't much to do anyway, and it's still too early to go see my little girl. My mother knocks softly and opens the door a crack before I've had a chance to answer. I see her eyes looking at me. "Good morning," I say, to signal that I'm awake.

"Good morning," she says, opening it some more. "The workers are here, and your father would like you to go up there and keep an eye on them."

"No problem. I'll be up in a minute."

The room is chilly. The ceiling is high and the walls thin and damp. "This has been the longest and rainiest winter in three decades" was a sentence we kept hearing over and over again on the weather forecasts. Winter was officially over, and we were in the middle of spring. I pull a sweater out of the bag I haven't even unpacked yet and go into the air-conditioned living room. My parents installed the air conditioner after we'd left home, and didn't see any point in opening a vent into the children's room. Just the living room and their bedroom. "Good morning," I say, and my father, sitting there with his cigarette and coffee, answers, "Good morning," without looking away from the screen. He's watching the Hebrew news, and when that's over, he zaps to Al Jazeera, where they have news all the time.

Breakfast is already waiting on the kitchen table. "Come to eat," my mother says. I look at my father and he looks at me. I know it's going to be difficult for the two of us to sit at the table together. My return must seem as odd to him as it does to me. "In a minute," he says, and I go and sit down at the kitchen table, in my regular seat, the one farthest away from Father, with my back to the TV, sipping tea with *naana* mint. The tea is too sweet. I had forgotten how sweet my mother makes it. It's a family rule, you drink tea with two spoons of sugar, coffee with none. There's no room for personal taste, it's a recipe handed down to her by her mother, who got it from her mother. "I don't eat breakfast," I explain, and she frowns in unmistakable sadness. "But I'll have something a bit later," I say. "In an hour or two."

Fifty steps separate my parents' house from the one where I am about to live. The noise of the floor-polishing machine rumbles in my ears even before I go inside. Today they're putting in the stairs. For over five years, there was just the outer shell. Only recently, after I'd announced that I was returning home, did my parents resume working on it, full steam ahead. It'll be ready pretty soon. In just a week, with any luck, or two at most, my mother said, and there's money too. My parents cashed in a savings account and they're putting it all into the house now, so I can move in. That's the way it is around here: good parents build homes for their children.

I walk into my future home, carrying a copper tray with two cups of tea for the men who are putting in the stairs. They turn off the machines for a moment. The one who seems to be in charge walks over to me, takes the tray and puts it down on the step he's just finished making. "Are you the owner?" he asks, and shakes my hand. "I'm Kamel." He gestures toward the younger guy, who puts down an enormous slab of marble and comes over to drink his tea. I study him and nod a greeting. He has a wide cleft all the way up from his lower lip to his nose. It doesn't look like an accident, more like a birth defect, and if he hadn't answered my greeting, I'd have assumed he couldn't talk. His voice is strange and squeaky, reminding me of the deaf kids' class at the far end of our elementary school. "Thanks for the tea," he says. His boss must be used to it by now, because he quickly makes a point of offsetting any apprehension or uneasiness I might be feeling. "Mohammed is an A-okay guy," he says. "We've been working together for two years. Like brothers, eh, Mohammed?" Mohammed lowers his head and tries to smile. I'm uncomfortable with the whole thing, slightly embarrassed even, as if we're dealing with some creature whose owner owes it to us to explain right away, before I panic, that he's just a harmless pet and not some wild beast, heaven forbid.

I'm going to have a big house, bigger than any of the rented homes I've lived in till now. There's no comparison. I try to persuade myself that the change might be for the better, that maybe I'll make it after all, that it might actually be nice to finally have a home of my own, considering that I've been dreaming of one my whole life. I walk up the stairs, to the floor where the bedrooms will be. The contractors have put in the marble slabs on that floor already. They have just one floor left, the one with the laundry room and the roof. The steps are a bit crooked, and some of them stick out. A few others broke as they were being installed. I don't know whether to say anything. To tell the truth, it doesn't really bother me much. I go into the bedroom. The walls haven't been painted yet. The en suite bathroom is all ready, and so is the one that will be for the children when the time comes. There isn't much more work to do, actually. Once the stairs are in, they'll put in the railing and then paint it all. The carpenter has put in the kitchen cabinets too, and he'll be installing the doors in a couple of days.

I won't even have to leave the house at all, I think, and have a cigarette in the bedroom. I won't even go to the grocery store. I'll just sit here at home, oblivious to everything. I could easily disappear, easily fix my life in such a way that nobody will know I'm back, nobody will notice I've come back to this lousy village. At least I have a big house to bury myself in. Wasn't it the oppressive feeling that I had run out of steam that made me come back here in the first place—a what's-the-point feeling that had been haunting me for the better part of a year and just kept getting worse? What was left for me in the big city anyway? Nothing, nada, just a sense of apprehension. I'd never felt secure there, even at home, and I don't intend to deceive myself into thinking that I'll feel any more comfortable

11

here. But at least I won't have to pay rent for a place to be apprehensive in.

The stairs man and his worker are at it again. I stand at the bedroom door and watch. "Hurry up, you idiot," the boss says, as he waits for the bucket full of brown slurry that the harelip with the submissive expression hands over to him. The whole scene makes me uneasy. The boss, who must be about my age, tries to make conversation, a big smile splashed across his face. "We never see you in the village at all. I was surprised to see you, and of course I know everyone your age around here. The younger generation, the children, I don't always know, because the village keeps getting bigger, but I know every single person your age. You must have studied in Germany. A doctor?"

I shake my head.

"So what did you study?"

"Journalism," I tell him.

"So you're a journalist?"

I nod.

"For the Jews?"

"Yes."

And soon enough I find myself getting into a conversation and breaking the promise I'd just made to myself a minute ago, not to make contact with anyone. How can I keep that up in a place like this?

"I'm telling you, there's no place like home. I've worked for the Jews too, and believe you me, even though you make a lot more money, it still feels different, you know what I mean, the way you come in every morning with the tea on a tray, with them you could be working for a week and they won't come near you. Not all of them. I'm not saying they're all like that. But now, with the things getting more and more tense and all, it's just getting worse. They can't tell the difference between people like us, living inside Israel, and the ones living on the West Bank. An Arab's an Arab as far as they're concerned. I bet you thought I was from the West Bank too when you came in and saw me in my dirty coverall. I bet you were scared," he says with a laugh.

Mohammed is standing there, and I hope he can't hear any of what we're saying. Maybe he's deaf after all. Our eyes meet and he quickly lowers his gaze as if I were a Border Policeman or who knows what. And the boss, who must have picked up on my discomfort and our mutual glance, smiles again and explains, "Don't pay any attention to the way I talk about him. Mohammed and I are like brothers, right, Mohammed?" He turns to him, and Mohammed smiles. "He's been with me for two years now. An excellent worker. And I look after him, take care of everything he needs, food and drink, and my old clothes so they don't stop him at the roadblocks. You know I could do time if they caught him in my car. I'm employing a ticking bomb, brother, a terrorist." He laughs. "Ask him. He can't live without me. Isn't that right, Mohammed?"

3

I t's late afternoon, and the traffic is heavier than I'd expected. New cars are cruising along. The cars are full, of young men, mostly. Almost all of them have two passengers in front and three in back, well dressed. The cars look like they've just been washed. I merge into the lane. Traffic is slow, especially on the main road of the village, where my wife's family's home is.

It's the hour when the high school lets out. That's how it was when I was a student, except that back then there would be lots of guys out looking for a bride, trying to impress the girls or use their only chance to see them close up, not from inside a car. I remember the dozens of guys waiting at the entrance to the school and joining the throng of kids streaming out.

The thought of it makes me smile, but the smile soon gives way to sadness, a fear that maybe I too, in my dirty old car, will be taken for one of the guys coming to impress the young girls. I've got to get to my in-laws' house already, damn it. I remember well how I used to look down on those guys. Some of them even came to school with cameras and shame-lessly took pictures of the girls they were interested in. They'd take snapshots so they could get the mother's approval before asking for the girl's hand. There were even more people at the gate to the junior high. Getting engaged to a very young girl was considered a greater achievement. Half the girls in the ninth grade were engaged, and if it hadn't been for the Israeli law, which doesn't allow marriage before the age of seventeen, they certainly would have gotten married before they were out of high school.

A girl who was properly raised was supposed to walk straight ahead and pretend not to notice if anyone honked at her, to move firmly forward without turning to look in either direction. The ones who turned to look were loose, and the ones who smiled as they did were regarded as a lost cause, practically sluts.

I steal a glance, a few small peeks so they don't suspect me of being one of the girl-watchers, and I see them, congregating at the edge of the road, older than children but barely into adolescence, looking different from what I'd expected. The boys look like Israeli high school students. Their clothes are so different from what we used to wear at their age, which was only ten years ago. Everyone wears jeans, everyone has gel in their hair, and their shirts are the latest fashion. When I was their age, we all dressed the same, in clothes that were made in the village, cotton pants and blue shirts. It wasn't until I'd been at the university that I happened to hear about brand names like Levi's or Nike or Lee Cooper. The designer men march along the right side of the road, and the girls along the left. The number of girls wearing a veil is even more surprising. I don't remember a single girl wearing a veil when I was at school.

It's unbelievable what ten years can do. Actually, I hardly recognize the place. I know a place that answers to the same name, I know faces that continue to be known by the same names too, but for some reason I don't really feel like I'm going back to an old familiar place. I'm going home, to a new place.

I greet my wife and she nods. Her mother is standing in the kitchen, which is right at the entrance, and when I hold out my hand, she extends her arm. Her hands are covered in oil. I shake her elbow. My wife's father is wearing pajamas with blue squares and brown stripes. He's sitting on a mattress, staring at the Arabic channel. He tries to get up to welcome me, but I hurry over to shake his hand so he doesn't have to go to any trouble. "The baby's asleep," my wife says, pointing to her parents' bedroom. I go in and look at her. How I've missed her, even though it's been just one day since we returned home. It's the first night I haven't slept in the same room as my little girl. The beds in my in-laws' bedroom are far away from one another. Twin beds, one on each side of the room. My daughter is on the bed on the western side. I fix the blanket that's covering her, and don't dare kiss her on the cheek, for fear she'll wake up and I'll be accused of harassment again.

The relations between my wife and myself could be described as delicate. Not that they were ever great, but somehow each of us managed to find the right space, the right position, so as not to get in the other's way. My wife didn't like the idea of returning to the village. In fact, she hated the idea, and she hated me all the more on account of it. On our last trip home from the city she said that if she'd known I'd wind up coming back home to the village, she'd never have agreed to marry me, and she added that the only reason she'd agreed to marry someone like me was to be far away from there. She didn't care that our economic situation was getting worse, that life in the city cost a fortune, to the point of becoming unbearable. The rent we were paying was dollar-linked and just kept soaring, till it amounted to more than half our joint income. And she wasn't all that bothered that it had become uncomfortable just to walk down the street. She was willing to put up with graffiti calling for her deportation, for her death. She didn't notice how our neighbors in the apartment building began looking at us differently, or else maybe she did notice but had decided to put up with it because of how much she loved the city, or rather, how much she loved being far away from the place where she'd been born. She didn't show any signs of concern when someone sprayed the wall of our building with ARABS OUT = PEACE + SECURITY. More than anything, she hated the village. She never explained exactly why, she just used to say, "You don't know the people there. You don't know what it's turned into." Since the day we got married and left the village together, she hasn't wanted to spend more than a day visiting there, no more than a few hours, in fact. The idea of sleeping over, either at her parents' or at mine, was out of the question, even though they kept begging her to stay, especially on holidays. Sometimes I got the impression there was some deep dark secret that explained why she detested the place so much, especially when she'd come out with such strange sentences like, "You have no idea what people there can do to anyone who isn't one of them," or "How would you know? If you were a woman, things would be different."

But I just couldn't stay in the city any longer. For two whole years I procrastinated about going back to the village. A little more than two years had gone by, actually, since everything started going downhill. I can recall the day when I was sent to cover the Arab demonstrations in Wadi Ara after the cabinet members put in an appearance at the al-Aqsa Mosque. I must have been the only journalist on the scene working for an Israeli paper, since as an Arab I had no trouble getting into the villages and standing around with the demonstrators, the only journalist who was actually standing on the side that the police and soldiers were aiming their guns at. I saw the injured being taken to the local infirmary, the masses of people huddling at the entrance to the small clinic, to see if their loved ones had been brought there, find out whether they were alive, whether they'd been injured. I was the only journalist who saw the fear in the eyes of the veiled women whose hearts would skip a beat every time someone was brought in, who would cry every time a shot was heard. I was there, and I knew that nobody had expected the police to react so harshly, so relentlessly. Like me, the demonstrators had always thought of themselves as citizens of Israel, and never imagined they would be shot at for demonstrating or for blocking an intersection.

Two days and more than a dozen casualties later, the riots were over. I went from funeral to funeral, from mourner to

mourner, interviewing parents as they wept and assigned blame
and expressed their horror. Then things calmed down. No more
tires were burned in intersections, there were no more rallies,
no more funerals, and life seemed to be going back to normal.
No more spontaneous outbursts like the ones that had cost the
locals so dearly. If only it could really have been over in two
days—but no, nothing has gone back to what it was before.
Ever since those days, something has been broken, something
has died. Two days of demonstrations had been enough for the
state to delegitimize its Arab population, to repudiate their
citizenship. Two days that only served to stoke the Jewish fires
of vindictiveness.

Those two days had changed my life. Suddenly my life as
an outsider, which had had its advantages, began to get in my
way. My being an outsider was what had qualified me for my
job and my position, and had given me the language in which
I was expert enough to work as a journalist. My being an outsider was beginning to put my life in danger. Even the place
where I worked, which I'd always considered a safe haven, had
changed. The report I submitted about those two days of demonstrations was the first to be changed beyond recognition, the
first story to occasion a meeting with my editor-in-chief, which
turned out to be more of a rebuke than a meeting. For the first
time I was being accused of having an axe to grind. "Next thing
we know, you'll be blocking the entrance to our offices and expecting us to applaud you," the editor said, laughing to put me
at ease. That was when I realized I was in the process of losing
my job. When I saw that the way they treated me depended on

the security situation, I began waiting for a letter of dismissal. It was just a question of time, and I knew I didn't really belong there anymore.

But I wasn't fired. The newspaper continued using me as a reporter in the West Bank, mainly because I was the only one who could deliver the goods, who could go into the Palestinian cities and villages and come back with stories. But ever since then they'd been keeping an eye on me. Every sentence I wrote was inspected, every word double-checked. I got used to being summoned by the editor-in-chief and being required to provide an explanation for every piece of information I submitted. I learned the rules soon enough, to steer clear of what people were saying and to focus on dry descriptions, sticking to the assignment, as I was told. I adopted the lingo of the military reporters: *terrorists, attacks, terrorism, criminal acts*. Some of the journalists in the Hebrew press—non-Zionist left-wingers— allowed themselves to lash out against the occupation and against the restrictions imposed on the Palestinian inhabitants, but I no longer dared. The privilege of criticizing government policy was an exclusively Jewish prerogative. I was liable to be seen as a journalist calling for the annihilation of the Zionist state, a fifth column biting the hand that was feeding it and dreaming each night of destroying the Jewish people.

I tried to survive. I'd always been a survivor. I knew how to adapt to my surroundings, working and doing what I wanted. Except that ever since those two bitter days in October, the task of survival had become tougher. I had to be twice as careful, to listen to quips and jabs by colleagues who'd never spoken to me like that before. I smiled when the secretary asked, almost every morning, "So, did you throw any stones in the entrance?" I smiled at the guard who inspected my bags at the entrance to our office building, I laughed when my colleagues talked about the self-indulgent Arabs who were living in Israel and had no idea what it was like when a combat plane is hovering over your house, when a tank heads right into your neighborhood. I laughed out loud, trying to conceal my discomfort, when we'd go out for a bite at the nearby restaurant and one of the others would invariably wink at the guard at the doorway and say, "Better frisk him carefully. He's suspicious." I said thank you every time someone told me that "Israeli Arabs really ought to say thank you." I agreed with my roommates when they criticized the Arab leadership in Israel, I denounced the Islamic Movement when they did, I expressed my grief over every Jewish casualty after a terrorist attack, I felt guilty, I cursed the suicide bombers, I called them cold-blooded murderers. I cursed God, the virgins, Paradise and myself. Especially myself, for doing everything I could to hold on to my job.

But I decided I'd had enough. Somehow I came to the conclusion that it would be much safer to live in an Arab village. Somehow it seemed to me that if I lived in a place where everyone was like me, things would be easier. I'd watch them get married and have children, and I'd feel more comfortable. I needed to return to a place, however small it might be, where Arabs didn't have to hide. Especially since so many people were returning anyhow. Very few were leaving, and apart from those who'd been banned, everyone would come back sooner or later.

I didn't see any point in telling my wife about my feelings. She'd never have understood.

I'm not going to stay with my in-laws for long. My wife and I hardly look at each other as I try to reassure everyone by telling them, as calmly as I can, about the feverish pace of the work being carried out on our house so it can be ready soon. When I finish, I don't dare repeat the invitation for my wife and baby to sleep over at my parents' home. My wife had objected to that idea even before we got here. She said she needs her privacy, and that she would feel uncomfortable in my parents' home, using the bathroom, for example. It was a declaration that seemed to me like a kind of punishment. I promise to come back to see the baby when she wakes up, and add that my parents have missed her and would also enjoy seeing her, so maybe I'd pick her up for a few hours in the late afternoon. "I've got to go now," I say. "I left the workers alone in the house."

4

I thought I heard some shots, a few rounds. Must be a wedding, or maybe it's the soldiers in Tul-Karm or Qalqilya, both close by. Even though it's just a village, the noise in this place is much louder than in the city. It's after midnight now, and the cruising cars never let up. You can hear them trying to go faster, revving up the motors, ignoring the makeshift speed bumps the neighbors put in, even though they're just forty or fifty feet apart, but the young drivers won't miss a chance to build up speed. The really loud screeching of tires, brakes being slammed and motors being pushed to the max are not quite as loud, since they come from a few blocks away, where there are no speed bumps and hardly even any buildings. That's just how it is. It's always been the younger generation's favorite form of entertainment. In the intermittent silences between cars I hear a hodgepodge of noises, some from television sets, some from people talking. I could swear I hear the sound of children playing. What is it with them, being up at such an hour? I remember when we were kids how we'd always show off about how late we'd gone to sleep the night before. I remember I'd always gone to sleep early, or to be precise, I'd always gone to bed early.

Tonight too, I've been in bed for two hours already. I was sure I'd fall asleep as soon as I shut my eyes. It had been a tough day. Everything was supposed to be finished by today. Tomorrow is our official moving-in day. Tomorrow I'll be sleeping with my wife and baby in our new house, together, the way families are supposed to. I don't know whether the thought reassures or terrifies me. First thing in the morning, my wife and mother-in-law arrived at the new house and started cleaning. Mother joined them, and the three of them spent the next few hours scouring the floor, removing spots of paint, not an easy job. I was in charge of various small but tiring jobs, like putting handles on the doors or hooks in the bathrooms or hanging curtains. I didn't get to the curtains, because the women needed me to dismantle windows and blinds so they could clean them and the frames underneath. Then I was supposed to put them back in. It isn't easy to remember which part of the window goes in first. Make even a small mistake and all your work will be wasted. I hated the windows and I couldn't understand why there should be so many in one lousy house.

Never mind, I'll hang the curtains tomorrow. It's just a matter of drilling a few holes and tightening a few screws. The tricky part is getting the measurements right and making sure the curtains are straight. Tomorrow we'll all be sleeping together, tomorrow our normal lives will be getting back on track. The week we both took off so we could move is over, and in two days we'll have to get back into our routine. Maybe that's what we need most right now: a routine that will put our lives in order, that will restore the proper rhythm of things, the natural flow. My wife will be teaching at one of the schools in the village and I'll be going back to the paper, half an hour's drive away from here, forty minutes at most. Tomorrow I'll take my wife's brother, Ashraf, to our old apartment to pick up some boxes we left behind. It's still ours. We paid rent on it till the end of the month, tomorrow.

5

My wife, my mother-in-law and my daughter arrive in the morning with Ashraf in the pickup he borrowed from one of his friends. By the time we get back with the boxes, they'll have finished cleaning. There isn't much left to do, just the floors, actually.

"Coming home?" Ashraf says, and sniggers. "Coming home to your birthplace, eh?" He and I get along pretty well, in fact. Not that we see each other very often. Every now and then he used to visit us and then stay for the weekend. Almost every time he came, we'd have a beer at one of the nearby bars. He finished college not long ago—economics—and after he gave up on finding a job in his field he started working in one of the mobile phone companies as a customer-service rep for Arab customers.

Dozens of workers are congregating in the village square, each holding a plastic bag. They lunge at every car that stops, hoping it may belong to a contractor or anyone else who's looking for cheap day laborers. Ashraf's pickup looks particularly promising. It reminds the workers of the contractors' pickups. When we stop at the intersection, to yield the

right-of-way to cars coming in the other direction, the workers converge on all the windows. I signal, with my hand and
my head, that we're not in the market for workers, but they
don't give up, and I hear them say things like, "Fifty shekels
for the whole day. Please." And, "Ten shekels an hour, any
job you want done." They don't let go of the car till it lurches
away and crosses the intersection. Ashraf goes on smiling. I
think that's how he overcomes the awkwardness of the situation. "Don't feel sorry for them," he says, and I'm not sure
who he's trying to convince—me or himself. "Now they're
begging, but deep inside they're convinced that every Israeli
Arab is a traitor and a collaborator."

On our way out of the village, the pickup joins a long line
of cars, dozens of them inching forward. "Another roadblock,"
Ashraf says. "Got your ID on you?" I nod, and he says, "Is this
what you're returning to? Believe me, I don't get it. How can
you return to a place like this for no better reason than to own
a bigger house? You don't know what you're coming back to,
my man. This isn't the place you left, when was it—ten, fifteen years ago?" He laughs again. "Did you hear the shooting
yesterday?" Little kids in cheap old clothes surround every car
that comes to a halt, some of them offering rags for sale, others chewing gum, lighters, sets of combs and scissors and packs
of tissue. As they approach Ashraf's pickup, he rolls up the windows and signals them to move away. "Do you have any idea
how much money they make?" he says. "They put on that pathetic face, and instead of going to school they come all the
way from Qalqilya and Tul-Karm on foot and beg. Every single

one of them makes at least a hundred shekels a day. I don't even make a hundred a day."

The pickup plods along and we can see the policemen at the roadblock. Ashraf says the people on the West Bank are the sorriest lot in the world, and he chuckles. "Ever since the Intifada, they have nothing better to do than to call us at work and give us an earful. That's how they pass the time of day, I'm telling you. They just call every service phone with a toll-free line. They can drive you crazy, and you have to be courteous, answer by the book, 'Cellcom at your service. This is Ashraf speaking. How may I help you?' Sometimes I feel like cursing them, cracking jokes with them, slamming the phone down in the middle of a call, but that's out, because they're always monitoring our customer-service calls. They keep dreaming up new ideas. This week, for instance, there was an onslaught of callers from Nablus. All of them want their phones to ring like one of Diana Haddad's new songs. Where am I going to find them a Diana Haddad ring tone now? In Jenin, they figured out this week that you could set your mobile to call from abroad too. Thousands called in, as if anyone is really going anywhere. They can't even get from Jenin to Nablus. They call just because they feel like it. Every time they hear there's a new service, they all call.

"Once this little girl phoned in and just sobbed away. I could hear the heavy shelling in the background and the little girl told me she was alone in the house, her father was out and she didn't know where he was. I have no idea how she wound up dialing my number. Maybe it was the last number her father had dialed. Makes sense. After all, they call Cellcom all day long. And there she is, crying, and I spend hours trying to reassure her. If they'd caught me, I'd have been fired on the spot, but I stay on the line with her till her father, or somebody, gets home when the shelling stops. I mean, you could actually hear the war in the background and you picture this kid all alone over there, scared to death, screaming, and me, like some military training officer, there I am telling her to get down, to take cover behind a wall, under a table. A military commander, that's what I was for her, I'm telling you," he says with a laugh.

As we approach the roadblock, we pull out our ID cards. The policeman glances at them and hands them right back to us. "Lucky they didn't ask us for licenses, 'cause this pickup isn't registered in my name and we'd never hear the end of it."

"Does this have to do with yesterday's shooting?" I ask. Ashraf laughs. "What makes you say that? They're just looking for some workers. So you heard the shooting yesterday? It was right next to our house, from a passing vehicle. Gang shooting. What's that to the police? They don't give a damn. All they care about is security stuff. But yesterday some guys I know must have come back drunk from some club in Tel Aviv and drove around our neighborhood. I was awake. I was standing on the balcony and I saw them. Suddenly one of them pulled out an Uzi and shot a few rounds. He must have been very happy. You'll get used to it."

Ashraf goes on laughing the whole way, telling me about my village, his village, the new village I no longer know, and his disdain is unmistakable from the word go. As we continue driving, he explains the best way to behave to avoid getting into trouble. "You're driving along a narrow road and a car comes in the opposite direction. There isn't enough room for both of you. You drive right back, *insha'Allah,* even if he only has to back up two meters and you have to do one hundred. Always back up, 'cause it could end in a shooting, depending on who happens to be in the car. You're driving along and two cars are blocking the road because the drivers are chatting through the open windows? Wait patiently. God help you if you honk. Just wait for them to finish their conversation. It won't take more than an hour, *insha'Allah.* Just wait and when they let you pass, smile and say thank you." Ashraf keeps laughing as he recites his survival lexicon. Then he explains that if they jump the line at the infirmary, I should just let it be. If I'm in line at the grocery shop and someone cuts in front of me, I should just stay cool. He swears that people have been killed in recent years because of things like that. Slowly his laughter dies down. "You have no idea what you're coming back to, do you?" he says, and his tone changes.

6

My wife gets into bed in the second-floor bedroom after putting the baby down in her crib, and I stay downstairs to watch TV, zapping till the news begins on the Israeli channel. I've got a satellite dish like everyone else around here, one hundred and ninety channels, more than ninety of them in Arabic, and one of the Israeli channels. The whole business of the Arab channels is pretty new to me, and I'm intrigued. I've never come across it before. When I left the village they were still using antennas, the kind that barely pick up the Israeli channel, and with any luck, a Jordanian one. I get a kick out of zapping, back and forth. I don't think I've ever spent more than five minutes watching the Arab channels. It's pretty amazing. There must be a dozen music channels with clip after clip showing half-naked Lebanese belly dancers. At first I can't believe Arabs would dress like that, just like on MTV. The songs come as a shock to me too, all of them seem the same and sound the same, about love, mostly, the same words, changing only slightly from one song to the next, the same rhymes, the same annoying melody, a pounding beat that I don't like at all. But still I stare at the dancing women, with their skimpy getups and undulating pelvises.

I keep on pressing the button with the up-arrow on it to switch channels. MTV is showing *Who Wants to Be a Millionnaire?* and Abu Dhabi has *The Weakest Link*. Soon enough I start skipping right over the religious channels. At first I thought they were cool, but now I see through them right away. Soon as I spot a sheikh with a head-cover, I know he's preaching or giving a religion lesson. There are countless channels like that, where they spend the whole day reading from the Koran and discussing what Islam does or doesn't allow you to do. I hate the look of the announcers, I hate the way they stress their *k*'s when they talk. It's something called Kalkala. I remember they told us about it in the seventh grade. You're supposed to enunciate the *k* very clearly when you're reading from the Koran, it's supposed to come straight from the throat like you're about to puke *kkkkk*. In one of those lessons, the teacher wanted to tell us about the heretics. "Who are the heretics of today?" he asked. Some students answered they were the people who put their faith in *al-asnam* (the idols), some said they were the sun worshippers, or those who believe in cows, or the murderers, or the Jews, but our bearded religion teacher didn't like any of those answers. In the end, he turned to the blackboard and wrote in gigantic letters: KARL MARX, and asked one of the kids to read what it said. The student overenunciated the *k* sound in *Karl* and the teacher gave him a beating to help him remember. Nobody understood what the hell Marx was. There are some channels, especially the official Saudi one, that are beneath contempt. Everything there seems different—the graphics, the music, the jingles. It's like the programs I used to watch on Jordanian TV a decade ago. It's amazing that in the age of cutting-edge television and state-of-the-art studios like Al Jazeera's and ones in Lebanon, they still have these backward channels with moderators who don't know the first thing about modern broadcasting. Everyone watches Al Jazeera when there's a new war on. Later, people get tired of it, because all the wars on television look the same lately. Someone had better come up with something new in the next war. We can't take it any-more, it's too boring staring at a black or green screen.

I'm not too crazy about Al Jazeera. From the little I can see, they spend hour after hour talking with experts and com-mentators, broadcasting news that everyone's heard already, news that most of the Arab world is used to hearing and likes to hear. They never mention the names of Arab leaders, never do any investigative reporting about rulers or important fig-ures in the Arab world. They don't want to upset anyone, least of all the oil magnates in the Gulf, with all their money—the money which, when all is said and done, pays for these chan-nels. It's pretty pathetic, really; the big name that the channel has made for itself is a hoax. It may be a revolution in the area of news coverage in the Arab world, but it still doesn't amount to real journalism.

I switch just in time to the news on Channel One, Israel TV, which begins with another item about a cell of Israeli Arabs who've been picked up on suspicion of helping a Palestinian suicide bomber get to Tel Aviv. Maybe my editor will ask me to do a story about it tomorrow. I feel like they've been phasing me out lately. Ever since the cutbacks and the decision that I'll go freelance and no longer be on the editorial board, I've hardly gotten any assignments. Maybe this time they'll need me, because everyone else is afraid of going into Palestinian villages, not only on the West Bank but in Israel too. I'm glad that cell got caught. Maybe it'll earn me something this month.

The doorbell rings. It's my mother and my two aunts, my father's sisters. "They're here in honor of our new house," my mother says.

"Welcome," I say. "My aunts are here," I answer my wife. The doorbell has awakened her and she wants to know who it is.

"Congratulations, *mabruk, ma-sha'Allah,* may this house be filled with children," they say, and drag their big selves inside. I pull along the two bags of presents they've brought us.

My wife comes down, trying not to show how annoyed she is at the unexpected callers. I hate it when she makes those faces, as if it's my fault, as if I want people to come visit us. "Where's the little one?" the older aunt asks her. "Asleep already? I was hoping to get a look at her."

"She's in her crib, you can take a look." My aunts follow my wife up the stairs. The two of them have trouble climbing, and the older one has to rest every other step, grasping the railing, panting, muttering, *"ya Allah,"* and taking another step or two. The younger one pauses every fourth step. Both of them complain about the stairs. Once they've taken a quick look at

34

the baby, they slowly make their way back down and settle into the armchairs in the living room, wiping their brows with the white kerchiefs they've been wearing, and trying to catch their breath. It takes quite a while till the older one manages to say, "She's adorable. Looks just like you," and the younger one adds, "May God bless her with a brother. Is there anything on the way? You need another one, and it's better for a woman to give birth while she's still young. I stopped having children at twenty-eight after I'd had eight. It's better for the woman, 'cause you never know when she's going to stop getting her monthly."

"Insha'Allah," my wife says diplomatically, and heads for the kitchen to get our regular guest kit, the one that all the villagers serve. A bowl of fruit, some nuts, cold drinks. Then she'll urge them to please help themselves, the way she's supposed to, and they'll have to eat or drink something, and toward the end of their visit she'll offer tea or coffee, a cue that it's time for them to leave. Tea and coffee must be offered even if they get up to go before you've had a chance. You're always supposed to say, "What? Leaving already? You haven't had your tea yet."

Nobody wants to mess with my aunts. You've got to make sure everything is done by the book. Otherwise, the attack will be particularly brutal. My wife knows this, and she's careful to do things the right way, except for that scowl that has me worrying that my aunts may catch on. "You needn't have bothered," they say, the way everyone does.

"The fact that you've bothered gives me strength," my wife replies, and passes the test with flying colors.

They're tough ladies, my aunts. Everyone in the village

knows it, and tries not to do anything that might make them angry. They're first-rate gossipmongers, great at bad-mouthing and criticizing anyone they don't like. In many ways, their impression of our house and of us is crucial to us.

After a few ritual exchanges and comments about the color of the kitchen cabinets, the railing and the sofa, my aunts get on my mother's case for letting my father, their brother, spend time in the café. "How do you allow it?" the younger aunt asks my mother. "He's a grandfather already, and still he spends time in cafés?"

"What can I do?" Mother says. "He goes there to spend time with his friends."

"What do you mean, what can you do?" my older aunt asks. "Stop him. What are you, a little girl? A man of his age and in his position? What does he think—that he's still eighteen? Sitting around all day playing cards and *shesh-besh*. I'll have you know that people have told me he gambles. They swore he plays for money. I wanted the earth to swallow me right then, I was so embarrassed. That's all we need—for worthless people to come and humiliate me because my brother spends his time playing cards in cafés. Why would he be playing cards when he has a good wife at home? My husband, *Allah yirhamo*, never spent a day in a café from the day we were married till the day he died."

"Instead of going to religion lessons at the mosque in the evening," my younger aunt says, "instead of sitting with good people, reading the Koran and praying, he'd rather sit around and smoke, drink coffee and play *tawlah*. What's missing in his life? Look at me. I recite verses from early evening until I fall asleep. Can there be anything better than reading verses to drive the demons and the evil eye away from your home and your children? It's all your fault, you make him run away."

My mother, experienced with such harangues, restrains herself as always, and makes do with nods and short replies, promising to do whatever she can. She will always pretend to agree with every word they say. She knows perfectly well that she has no choice and that no matter what she does they'll never think well of her and will never stop making fun of her or criticizing what she does.

My older aunt tells us about another man she knows who "brought a bride from the West Bank." The brides from the West Bank are a subject of conversation, and they mention a long list of middle-aged men who "brought brides from the West Bank." "An eighteen-year-old," my older aunt says of her new neighbor. "Adorable, sweet, white as an angel, not like the monster he had who just kept getting fatter and fatter."

The younger aunt agrees. "I wish my sons would each bring a bride from the West Bank. There's nothing better than having children, and today's girls don't want to have so many." It takes me a long time to realize that taking a second wife from the West Bank is becoming the norm in our village. Because the girl is from over there, they can disregard the Israeli prohibition on polygamy. "It's just because they don't want the Arabs to multiply," my older aunt says. "It goes against the teachings of Islam." As far as the young brides from the West Bank are concerned, marrying an Israeli Arab, no matter how old, is a chance to escape from poverty, especially since the *mohar* gift the Israeli grooms are willing to pay is a windfall for the relatives who stay behind.

My aunts crack sunflower seeds, and the more the conversation picks up, the faster they crack them. Their talk is animated, as they review the village gossip and compare versions. They talk of a man who stabbed his brother last night. One of them heard about fifteen stab wounds; the other, who insists that her source is more reliable, heard it was eighteen. They talk about men who cheat on their wives, about how they were caught and where and when. They talk about homes that have been robbed recently, how much was taken from each house, who the suspects are, what weapons they used—an Uzi, a .36 or a .38—like regular small arms experts.

My mother must have heard my aunts' stories already. My wife shows some interest, and every now and then, whether out of politeness or out of genuine concern, she gets in a question of clarification like, "Are you talking about the brother of so-and-so?" My wife knows the people around here much better than I do, and her reactions give the impression that she's not surprised at the shocking stories that come up in the conversation and takes them in stride. I'm the only one who sits there and can't believe things like that are happening around me. My aunts go on to describe how children are being kidnapped for ransom on their way home from school, how people get shot, even when they're just sitting in a café. How a week ago a guy drove up on a motorbike and walked in with his helmet still on and a pistol in his hand, and shot someone. "And what would have happened if my brother had been sitting there that minute?" my younger aunt asks my mother. They talk about little children who've been raped, businesses that have been burgled and youngsters who've been arrested.

My aunts stay for a long time, and finally say, *"Y'Allah,"* and get up to leave. My wife urges them to have some tea. First they say they can't but she skillfully insists and makes them promise not to leave before tea is served. They stay seated on the sofa and I can tell by the look in their eyes that they're satisfied with my wife's behavior.

By the time the tea arrives, I have heard more stories— about usurious moneylenders using thugs who don't think twice about shooting anyone who's behind on his payments, about a whole army of criminals who exact protection payments from businesses and rape the wife of anyone who turns them down, or force them out of their vehicle in the middle of the village and confiscate it in broad daylight like the tax authorities, and about one poor guy, owner of a grocery store, who balked and dared to cross them. His store was sprayed with submachine-gun fire and now he pays them like everyone else does.

When they leave, they kiss my wife and again wish her well in the new house, and say how they hope Allah will sow blessings in her home and in her womb. My wife clears away the refreshments tray. I turn the TV on again and watch an Arab news channel. Before my wife goes back up to the bedroom I ask her whether those stories are true. She sniggers and says that it's all they talk about in the teachers' room all day. "What would you know? Just coming back here to sleep. You don't work here like me. I'm the one who got screwed by moving back here. What do you know about things anyway? You still think the teachers hit the pupils, don't you? Don't you understand it's the other way around now, that the teachers are scared, even in elementary school? That teachers have been stabbed? You've brought me back to a place where you ask kids at school what they want to be when they grow up and without batting an eye, half the class say they want to be gang members."

7

I hardly write for the paper anymore now. Cutbacks, they say. Less than a year ago, I had a position and a contract. My name was featured at the top of the masthead with the other members of the editorial board, and now it appears under the heading "regular contributors." In a lousy month I don't get more than ten small items into the paper. But still I keep going there each morning. It's become a bit embarrassing lately. My spot with the computer has been given to a perky young fashion reporter. I don't have a desk either, but I go there anyway. I want them to see me, to remember that I still exist, that I'm still ready to do my bit for that shitty rag. Mostly I sit in the smoking room going through the papers, turning pages till around noon, then make the rounds of the nearby streets. I never eat out anymore. On rare occasions I allow myself to sit in a café and order a short espresso, and then I usually spend at least an hour sipping it, browsing through the papers.

For the first time in my life, I've begun looking at the financial supplements before the other sections. Stories about mass layoffs, bankruptcies, the poverty line, the monthly unemployment figures reassure me to some extent. The Arab towns and villages have always held the lead on those unemployment and poverty ratings, and for me this has been a comfort of sorts. My wife and I are managing okay for now. The return home salvaged the situation, and was actually the smartest step I could have taken. We don't have all that many expenses, don't even spend much for food, because we eat at our parents' houses. We can really make ends meet on my wife's salary alone, even though teachers' salaries are among the lowest in the country, or perhaps the very lowest.

Last month I got four hundred shekels for the only story of mine that got published all month. And even then, my editor made a point of reminding me that "for a story like that I normally pay two hundred."

I'm dumbfounded at all the want ads in the supplements, considering the constantly rising unemployment rate. I've been reading the ads very closely lately. I started by looking for a position as a reporter, a proofreader, a copy editor. Anything as long as it has to do with journalism. But no go. Every now and then when I'd go back to the paper, I'd phone the people who'd placed those ads looking for energetic youngsters in search of an interesting job, and for whatever reason one phone call was enough for them to decide I wasn't right. In the beginning I rang some of the ones looking for young academics or stipulating that the job was "suitable for a student." I'd send in a résumé without even knowing exactly what the job was, but I never got a reply.

Nobody in my family knew what I was going through and I saw no point in telling them for the time being. Including my wife. Every day I'd leave the house early in the morning and head for the paper, only to return in the afternoon pretending to be this exhausted guy coming home from a hard day's work. My wife did notice that I no longer had any full-length articles and that my name hardly appeared in the paper, but I told her that I'd been promoted to the news desk and that I was now responsible for several of the reporters covering the West Bank. What I'd really been given was the job of a rewriter, a kind of subeditor whose main job is to train new reporters, and all I write are items that require a lot of experience, the kind that can't be assigned to beginners. We haven't begun to feel the loss of my salary yet. The real deterioration only began last month and we haven't noticed it yet because our expenses are so negligible. But I know things can't continue this way. I can't go on fooling everybody. I've got to find another job. I'll keep doing whatever I can to make sure my name does appear in the paper occasionally, but I've got to find another source of income. I can't pretend to be working, I can't continue going there every morning. I've got a feeling that pretty soon one of the guys in charge is going to ask me diplomatically to stop. I know that my coming there actually upsets some of the people, but above all it upsets me.

I've got to look for the kind of job that someone like me has a chance of getting. If need be, I'll work in construction. I know it will be tough at first, but I'm sure I'll get used to it. Who said the solution has to be construction, though? I bet I could find a job caring for an invalid. They always want Arabs for those. An old person, maybe, or retarded. That would be the best solution as far as I'm concerned. Nobody needs to know about my new job. Nobody in my family will have to feel humiliated. I can't afford not to work. I can't afford to find myself without a livelihood. I want everything to go well here. I know how important that is to everyone.

People around me are forever discussing the money that others have. I don't know whether it's deliberate or not, but almost every time I come to visit they start talking about how this one's son or that one's son built a thirteen-hundred-foot home. My mother-in-law is taking an interest in houses, and sometimes I think she's compiling a list of every person who's building something—where it is and how much it's costing. She spends a lot of time on cars too, and always has tales to tell about relatives who've bought a new Mercedes or a Volvo or a Jeep. She knows when women in the village started to take driving lessons, how many they've taken and how many driving tests they had to take before getting their licenses. The stories I hear at my in-laws' home in the evenings about people with a lot of money certainly don't jibe with all those stories and figures in the business supplement I read in the mornings. I'm mystified at how people can just go on building and buying new cars when the situation is so bad. I never hear any stories about poor people who can't even build a single room for when they get married. All I hear in my in-laws' home are great success stories. Sometimes my mother-in-law makes a point of mentioning, as she describes yet another young man who built a house and bought a shiny car for his fiancé or his new wife, that he had once asked for her daughter's—my wife's—hand in marriage, but they had turned him down. Her voice is sad as she tells me this, and it makes me feel very uncomfortable, especially in the presence of my wife, who doesn't say a thing. Sometimes my mother-in-law says, "I suppose she was young then, and we're not like everyone else. We wanted her to finish school first. She was good at school and we didn't want her to just get married and stay at home."

My father-in-law, on the other hand, specializes in real estate and livelihoods. He knows who has bought land from whom, how many acres the deal covered, how much money changed hands and which lawyer handled the transaction. He knows how much certain people make per day, per week, per month and per year. He never mentions people's education. Educated people aren't that interesting to him. He values people by their income. He can spend a very long time calculating, for instance, how much the barber at the shop across the street makes in a year. He counts the people coming into the shop, at least forty a day, and nearly a hundred on weekends, not to mention the *Id el-Fitr* and *Id el-Adha* holidays, and haircuts for grooms, which cost almost three times as much as a regular cut. He calculates the wages the barber pays, the expenses, scissors, machines and various scents and lotions, and establishes firmly just how much he makes each month. *Minimum* is the word he uses to conclude his findings concerning people's incomes. He admires garage owners who've made it big, and moving-company owners, money changers, building contractors and the proprietors of hardware stores, shoe stores and clothing stores.

PART TWO

"There's Some Kind of Roadblock at the Entrance"

1

The paper hasn't arrived. The paperboy must have skipped us again, or maybe he's sick. I'm suddenly uneasy about the fact that I've never actually seen the paper route guy. I switch on the TV and turn up the volume, but don't sit down to watch. My wife is still upstairs, getting herself and the baby ready to leave. "Is the milk ready yet?" she shouts from above.

"Yes," I lie, and quickly pour the formula into the bottle and shake it.

I smile at the baby, who's coming downstairs in her mother's arms. "Good morning," I say to her, and approach with the bottle in my hand, but first I kiss her on the cheek. My wife will give the baby her bottle now, and I'll go upstairs, with my coffee in my hand, take a few sips, light a cigarette and take a few puffs, put it out under the faucet and throw it in the garbage, sit on the toilet, and when I'm through I'll look and check the result. Then I'll quickly brush my teeth, wash my face, change and come downstairs. I'll talk to my daughter again and try to smile at her. I'll say good morning all over again, and she'll smile back—or not. I'll take my briefcase from the study on the bottom floor and check how much cash I have in my wallet to see if it's enough.

I'm ready now. I pick up the baby. According to the weather report at the end of last night's evening news, it's going to be warmer than usual today. My wife sighs. As far as I'm concerned, it doesn't really matter. First we'll stop at the nursery where we've begun leaving the baby. Every morning when we hand her over she cries, and we're both kind of sad because of it, but we have no choice. My wife has to go to work, and for now at least, so do I. Then I'll take my wife to the elementary school where she teaches. We'll say good-bye, she'll ask when I'm coming home and I'll say I can't tell because it depends on what happens today. Sometimes, when there's a terrorist attack or a major military operation, I stay out longer and walk around because it's only logical that a deputy news editor would be busy on days like that. I hope nothing out of the ordinary happens today. Sometimes those aimless amblings in the city streets are extremely awkward. I try not to walk the same streets twice, to keep changing locations. It isn't only my family and the people in the village that I'm ashamed of facing because I've lost my job, but strangers too—kiosk owners or people in the café that I've never even met. So I try not to pass by them too often, because I don't want them to think of me as a loafer.

I turn on the car radio and decide I've got to put an end to it, to the disgrace of it. Things can't go on this way. If another week goes by without my finding a new job, I'll have no choice but to go to the Unemployment Office and apply for benefits. Nobody needs to know yet. I could go on leaving the village every morning. I'll go to an office far away where they don't have any Arabs at all.

2

Something's wrong. At this hour, the cars are all supposed to be heading out of the village to work, but they're driving in, and some of the drivers coming toward me are flashing their brights. Right away, I check if my seat belt's fastened. Flashing brights mean there's a police roadblock at the exit.

The closer I get to the main road out of the village, in the direction of the nearby Jewish moshavim and kibbutzim and, beyond them, the cities, the heavier the traffic. Drivers are honking nervously, trying to turn around and creating a traffic jam. I manage to find a spot to park the car on the shoulder, get out and quickly march toward the exit, where hundreds of people have gathered. "Is it true?" asks a young man who's also hurrying in the same direction.

"Is what true?"

"That they've sealed off the village?"

I don't know how to react. I try not to laugh in his face, try not to seem like a know-it-all. "We'll find out soon enough," I say, and add, *"Allah yustur,"* to make sure I sound like I belong. With every second that goes by, the crowd at the exit just keeps growing. Mostly they look disgruntled, and worried about the day's wages they're about to lose. I recognize many of the faces and realize that some of them are people I know personally.

"What's happening?" some of the people I know ask, turning to me. I'm the journalist in this village, after all, and they're hoping I might have some idea of what's going on. I shrug. Inching my way to the front of the crowd, I make out remarks like, "All the exits are blocked," "Some people tried to make it by the dirt roads, the ones the tractors use, but they couldn't get through," and a story about one of the workers who tried to approach the soldiers and took a bullet. They say the bullet was shot with intent to kill, because his arm was right above his chest when he was hit. As I get closer, I notice that two tanks are blocking the road about five hundred feet away from the crowd, and aiming their enormous barrels at the people below. Everyone turns in the direction of the tanks, the jeeps and the soldiers, except for the mayor, who stands there with his back to the soldiers, facing the villagers and begging them to stay back. The mayor keeps explaining that he found out about the blockade only that morning and he has already called the people in charge, who promised to get back to him and to take care of it at once. He goes on to say that there must have been some mistake, urges the crowd to be patient, to wait a while till it all blows over. "You'll make it to work today," he promises. "Just give me a chance to find out what's happening."

"The soldiers must have confused us with Tul-Karm," someone blurts out, and manages to elicit some laughter. Many rolls of barbed wire are blocking the road. I look in either direction and discover that they stretch as far as the eye can see. Someone in the crowd swears that the wire runs around the entire village, and wonders just when the soldiers had a chance to roll out so much. In the distance we see that besides the tanks blocking the road there are others scattered in the fields, evenly spaced on either side of the road. The tanks are still, but their engines are running, giving off billows of smoke every now and then as the roar of the engines grows louder.

3

What's going on here damn it? We've had road-blocks at the entrance and exit of the village almost every morning, but this is something altogether different. This new turn of events scares me at first, then makes me happy for a few minutes. I'll finally have a good story, I think. When's the last time they used tanks against Arab citizens? A story like that even has a chance of being printed on the front page and, who knows, maybe it will lead to my being invited for a radio interview, like in the good days. I'm right on the spot, after all, in the heart of the story—a journalist and a resident of the besieged village. I might even get asked to appear on TV. I've been on a few current-events programs, to the delight of my family and friends, even my in-laws. I've always enjoyed it when one of the research assistants asked me to come to the studio. I enjoyed how they'd send a cab to pick me up, I enjoyed dressing nicely and getting made up. It was usually just one of the morning or late-night shows, but still, my TV moments were the best I'd known. Maybe these tanks would bring them back.

I work my way back out through the front rows of the crowd, trying to move away so I can update one of my editors about what's going on. The way back into the village is becoming more and more jammed. All those who'd tried to get to work through the side roads are making their way back now that they've realized all the roads are subject to the same fate. There's no doubt about it now: the village is blocked off on all sides.

I left my mobile in my briefcase in the car. I glance at my watch and see it's almost eight. I step up my pace so I can catch the morning news on my car radio before phoning the news desk at the paper. There's no more honking or bottlenecks now. Apparently the news has spread. People have parked in the middle of the road. Where can they go anyway?

The news makes no mention of what's happening in the village. They talk about cities on the West Bank, cabinet meetings, the rising exchange rate of the dollar, but nothing to do with Israeli Arabs. Maybe it's a mistake after all, as the mayor said, I think as I dial the paper. But luckily for me, even a mistake like that is still a story, for the back page, maybe, where they put the most amusing items.

The switchboard operator is nice as she takes my call. She says good morning, asks how the baby's doing and only then lets me know that the editor-in-chief hasn't arrived yet. I decide to phone him on his mobile. I was one of the paper's senior writers until not long ago, after all, and the events in this village are an emergency situation. The editor answers from his car. He sounds surprised at what I tell him, and tries to see if

I'm not pulling his leg. "Tanks? Bulldozers? Are you kidding?" he says with a laugh.

"I'm telling you they've shot someone already. I mean, I have to check it out first, but it's a closure, and it's worse than anything I saw in Ramallah or Nablus or Jenin. It's more like Gaza. They've sealed off one hundred percent of the village," I tell him.

4

The call to my editor is cut off. "Hello ... Hello ..." I'm not even sure he heard my last sentence. For a moment I think maybe he cut me off deliberately, but he wouldn't pull such a thing on me. It's not as though I call him all the time, and he knows I wouldn't dare call him unless it was important. I try calling again, and get a recorded message: "Thank you for using Cellcom. The subscriber you have called is temporarily unavailable."

The phone is out of order. At least it wasn't the editor who cut off the call. Must be a technical problem. They'll fix it right away. Sometimes when you're under a power line or something like that, there's no reception. I'll wait a few minutes, and then I'll dial again. But the phone is still dead. I get out of the car and turn to one of the people walking toward the crowd. "Excuse me," I say with a very appreciative expression. "Excuse me, would you happen to have a phone? Mine's dead."

The guy nods and pulls a phone out of a leather pouch attached to his pants. He hands it to me and asks, "What's going on in the village?" without seriously expecting an answer, just trying to make conversation. "I don't know," I say, and turn on his phone, but I get the same announcement. "Your line's dead too," I say, smiling. "Must be a technical hitch at the company." The guy tries for himself. "*Wallah*, that's strange, first time it's ever happened."

It could still be a technical problem. Maybe the lines are jammed or maybe there's been some catastrophe. On days when there's a terrorist attack, cellular exchanges crash. It happens all over the country. I'll go back home and call from there, I think. Except that my car is stuck in the middle of the road among dozens of others and it will take an hour for them to move now. Everyone is waiting for the roadblock to be removed so they can get to wherever they were going outside the village.

I'll call from the bank, I think. My older brother's the manager of one of the departments there. I'll go into his office and phone. They've got to send a photographer in right away, before those damn tanks pull out. Without a good picture, I can forget about a cover story. The bank is very close by, a few minutes' walk from the edge of the village. The commotion and the traffic jam just keep getting worse. People are pacing back and forth without the slightest idea what they're doing or what's happening. They talk among themselves, registering surprise and some concern and mainly agitation and impatience.

"What's happening?" my brother asks as I enter the bank. "I heard there's a roadblock at the exit from the village. Anything wrong?"

"I don't know," I tell him, and follow him toward his little office with the metal blinds. His office is empty, and the bank is pretty empty too. It's still early in the morning, and except for two older women leaning on the teller's counter there are no customers yet. My brother has hung a picture of himself with the deputy manager of his bank, not of the branch, but of the entire bank. My brother, in a white hospital gown, lying in bed, an IV in his left arm and his right hand shaking the deputy manager's, with both of them smiling at the camera.

The deputy manager had come to visit after my brother was shot. The bank has been robbed countless times, but he was only shot at once. One of the robbers got edgy because there wasn't enough money in the till and he took a shot at my brother, who was standing behind the counter. He was lucky, everyone said, just one broken rib. The bullet missed his heart by a few millimeters. Usually they shoot in the air or spray the windows with bullets. My brother was in the hospital for a few days, had some operations and recovered. A miracle, everyone said, a miracle from God. After that, he changed a lot. He became more religious, started fasting on Ramadan, praying at home and then going to the mosque too, and not just on Fridays. His wife also started praying. To tell the truth, she started before he did, on the day he was shot, in fact. The first time it was in the hospital, in the lobby outside the intensive care unit where my brother was. He joined her only after he left the hospital. But they're not completely religious. I mean, he does pray, but he can also go swimming in a bathing suit, and his wife doesn't wear the veil, or even cover her head with a colored scarf. But that's only because she's still young. Someday she'll start wearing a veil too, like her mother, like my mother.

"My mobile phone's gone dead," I tell my brother. "Can I use yours?"

"We don't have a connection either," my brother says, and presses the speaker. The busy tone echoes through his office.

5

I check my phone again, and it announces that the line is still disconnected. I breathe heavily as I march back from the bank toward my parents' home. I'm beginning to feel the stress. To think, I finally have a juicy story, and now I can't even make contact with the paper. And what kind of a story is this anyhow? If it were all a mistake, they would have fixed it by now. Besides, what kind of a mistake could cause the army to send such large forces in and to seal off the village?

I'm beginning to feel like a jerk. I've got to calm down. Nothing's happened. I'm jumping to conclusions again. My fears are getting the better of me and sapping my common sense. What am I so worried about? It's just a fucking roadblock, that's all, and maybe it's nothing more than a drill, or maybe they've had warnings of a Palestinian terrorist cell hiding in the village? Why a cell? I bet it's just a single person. Maybe they have information about a serious operation and the soldiers can't take any chances. And maybe the whole thing is over by now and people are already on their way to work, the way the mayor promised. When am I going to stop acting like a child? I hope I didn't overdo it with my older brother.

I'll go home now. There's no point going back to the car, because everything's blocked and there's no way I'll be able to get the car out till the others start moving. It's the first time I've walked such a distance within the village since I came back. I hardly go anywhere on foot. The only walk I take is from our house to my parents' house next door. I hardly leave that area if I can help it, not even to go to the grocery store. I try to get my wife to go instead. Sometimes I have no choice and I do find myself in the center of the village, on Baghdad Street next to Saladin Square. They've started naming the streets and squares here lately. Sometimes I go to the pharmacy or buy a falafel or some cookies or fruit.

In the evenings, the village center is packed with cars and people and there are dozens of youngsters on the town hall steps, smoking and cracking sunflower seeds. From a distance, it looks as if they're not even talking to one another, just staring at the cars going by. The cars in the center move slowly, aimlessly. People just cruise around in their cars and greet one another, roaming about and studying the passersby. I hate being visible, because I know how they stare at me. Who is this guy anyway? Does he live in this village?

This is no place for strangers. Not that I'm a stranger; I was born here and spent eighteen years of my life here. But still, there are rules. Initially, when I'd bump into people, I'd try to look away, to pretend I hadn't seen them, but lately I've started studying them, looking at them the way they look at me, and sometimes I spot a familiar face or find myself smiling at someone peering at me from a passing vehicle, remembering that we'd been in school together, and I wave automatically. I've taken to greeting every familiar face with *salam aleikum* too, regardless of whether I can place the person or remember his name and what relationship we had, if any. Even though I don't leave the house much, I realize that from week to week, from day to day, I recognize more and more faces. I know that the number of times I say *salam aleikum* is growing by the day. These things happen and I have no control over them.

It hasn't been long since we moved back here, but I can go into stores in the village center without being questioned, as if I've been shopping there all along. People are less suspicious. Some of the salespeople recognize me by now and greet me when I walk in. The first time I went to buy a falafel, for instance, the vendor didn't ask me a thing. He just looked at me, studied me and decided I was a stranger. I tried to be polite, the way a stranger ought to be. The second time he felt he could ask me whether I was a local. When I said I was, he wanted to know whose son, what I did for a living, whether I knew so-and-so, who my wife was, whose daughter she was, what she did. The third time, he felt he could inquire how much I made at the paper and how much my wife made as a teacher. I lied. The figures I gave were much too high. Twice the highest salary I ever made at the paper when I was on the editorial board. I could afford to lie, about journalism at least. Nobody has a clue how much a journalist makes. When it comes to teachers, on the other hand, everyone knows the answer.

I don't like being questioned this way by salespeople, some of whom are half my age. I've never asked anyone how much he or she makes a month, it's been more than ten years since I've discussed my personal life with a salesperson and I've almost forgotten how it goes here. Other salespeople or just people who happened to be waiting in line at the bank or the pharmacy or the infirmary, as soon as they find out who I am, also want to know what I've been doing all these years, what it was like to live in a Jewish city. Did I have any male children? Almost invariably, the people who interrogated me declared that coming back to the village was a smart move. They found it hard to understand how anyone could live anywhere else. They looked at me as if I were an alien and congratulated me on my decision to return. "Is there anything better than living among your own? With your family?" was something I heard over and over again.

I hate those situations, and I sometimes get annoyed at my wife for making me do the kinds of chores that force me to keep going down to the center and to bump into people. I'd prefer for her to do those things instead, but I know it would be considered odd. Fact is, I've never seen a woman at any of those stores, and if there were any, she was usually there together with her husband or a male relative. An Arab woman would never go out to buy hummus or falafel on her own. It was unthinkable. The first time I was made to go down to the center of the village, it was to fix my wife's wedding ring. One of the stones had fallen out three weeks earlier, and I couldn't procrastinate any longer. She just went on and on about that stone and that ring. She said it was a bad omen, that the damage to the ring was mostly a sign that there was something wrong with our marriage, which was falling apart. I reached the iron gate. I tried to push it in, but in vain. The gate was locked. The salesperson sitting on the inside looked at me, tilted his head forward, and through the loudspeaker of the intercom next to the gate I could hear him ask, "Who are you?" Only after I gave him my name, my father's name and my last name did he smile and press the button and signal me to push the gate, which gave off a squeaky sound. Another iron gate came next, but so long as the first one was not completely shut, he didn't press the button that would open the second one. For a few very scary seconds I was locked in a steel cage. This place must have been robbed a million times, I thought.

"Ahalan u-sahalan," the salesperson greeted me, getting up and taking my hand. "I've heard about you. You just returned to the village a short while ago, right? You may not know this, but your father and I used to be close friends. Nowadays, because of business, we hardly see one another, but he's like a brother to me." The salesperson looked my father's age. His large head was covered with white hair and his enormous body filled the pink director's chair on the other side of the counter. All of the gold in front of him was yellow, shiny. On the back of the chair he had placed a green prayer mat with two mosques depicted on it. In his one hand he shifted the beads on his *masbakha* as he inquired about me and my wife, expressed his approval of our return and asked how he could help. I handed him the ring. He said it was nothing, he could fix the damage on the spot, in just a few minutes. My parents had bought the ring from him. He told me they had bought the jewelry for my brother's wedding from him too. "I have the best merchandise

anywhere around here, and I gave your father a great price, same as I'd give my own brother."

The wedding jewels replaced money as the groom's *mohar* payment, and represented a pretty big expense for the groom's parents. The salesperson felt obliged to note that my parents had not skimped and had bought the most expensive ones. Both for my wife and for my older brother's. "I want you to know," he said, "that your parents are exceptionally fair. They bought your wife the very same things they bought for your older brother's wife, and it's only a wise person like your father who'd do that, because you know how it is, women look at one another and get jealous. They did the smart thing. They asked for the identical set for your wife. I had to place a special order." He laughed. Me he'd never seen before, maybe when I was little, he said. But he saw my father and my older brother in the mosque every Friday. "Tell me," he asked as he handed me back the ring, "which mosque do you pray at?"

"At home," I muttered. "I pray at home."

"I guess you haven't had a chance to get to know the mosques around here. I'm telling you, come to our mosque, together with your brother. That would be the best. We don't have a lot of politics, or a lot of fanatics. I know your family, it's what would suit you best. Your family are like us, not like some of those crazies."

Yesterday, two more stones fell out of the wedding ring, the one I had fixed recently, and another one. My wife wants me to go have it fixed again, even though she figures it probably won't hold.

6

I pass by the mosque, which means I'm back in my own neighborhood already. The older people at the entrance don't seem the least bit worried. Rolling their Arab tobacco and licking it tight, huddling there together all day waiting for the next prayer hour. What else do they have to do, actually? At least they don't feel alone, and they can spend hours talking about people who died two thousand years ago. I blurt out a *salam aleikum* to which they respond with an *aleikum salam*, and I raise my hand. I've got to calm down. Truth is, I'm much calmer already. Some bulldozer must have slashed a cable and all the mobile phones went dead because the lines were jammed. Maybe an antenna has been damaged. Everything will be all right. Maybe I shouldn't go to my parents', maybe I ought to check the exit first, see if the roads are open already and retrieve my car. People in the street don't seem to think it's anything serious. There's cheerful music inside the houses, Egyptian pop. I recognize it and it makes me happy, even though, on the whole, I hate the trend. Every now and then, a car drives by and brakes just before the makeshift speed bumps that were put there to deal with reckless young drivers and car thieves who like to show off their loot by racing through the streets at crazy speeds. Some of the neighbors simply poured cement down in the shape of a small mound opposite the house, while others preferred to slow things down by digging a ditch from one side of the road to the other. Housewives are mopping the house and pouring the dirty water into the street, the way they do every morning. Where on earth, I ask myself, did I get the idea they were closing off the village?

My parents' home is the first one on the northern edge of the village, then my older brother's, then mine. The two brothers' houses look exactly the same, and on the remaining piece of land they'll build the fourth house, identical to ours, for my younger brother when he finishes school. All his life, my father has loathed fights over land, especially among brothers, which is why he made sure, long ago, to divide it up evenly among us. "So nobody says I gave one more or less than the rest," he tells us. I don't think my parents have heard anything about what's going on. I'll tell them I overslept and that I just came to say good-bye on my way to work. "Good morning," I say, and they both answer. My mother is preparing something in the kitchen and my father is sitting on the pink sofa staring at another newscast on Al Jazeera. They don't seem surprised to see me, despite the unlikely hour of my visit. My father sits up to greet me. "What do you think?" he asks me "Have they arrested anyone yet? What do they want anyway?"

"I hope God takes the lot of them," my mother says, and wipes off the counter. "Hungry?"

"Not really. Maybe I'll have a bite a little later," I say. So my parents do know, and I try to check whether it's because of something they saw on TV, because they couldn't possibly have gone out yet. Where would they be going, anyway?

But none of the events in the village has been mentioned on television. My heart starts beating hard again, and I try to keep my body from trembling when my mother curses the Jews and says they'd almost had a heart attack the night before when someone came banging on their bedroom window at about three A.M. "Who could be knocking at such an hour?" my mother says. "We were sure something terrible *la samakh Allah* had happened to one of you or your children."

It was my younger brother. He'd knocked on the door first, and when they didn't hear him he knocked on their bedroom window, right over their heads. My younger brother was dead tired. My father says they could hardly make sense of what he was saying about what had happened, except that the security guards at the student dorms had come with the Border Police, had ordered all of the Arab students out of their rooms and had escorted every one of them home.

"Where is he?" I ask at once, shouting, even. "Where is he?" And my mother asks me to pipe down, because my younger brother is asleep. "Poor boy," she says, "they kept them up all night." I hurry into the room where my younger brother is sleeping, the room we once shared. I move the old door slowly, trying to keep it from squeaking in its frame. I look at him, his thin, long body stretched out on the bed. The bedspread he'd covered himself with has fallen off. I'm about to cover him, but then I realize it's too hot for that. I notice I'm perspiring. I close the door again and hurry out. "I'm going out for a while. I'll be back soon," I tell my parents, checking their phone on my way out to see if it's working. It isn't. "It's dead," my father says. "Want something to eat?" I hear my mother ask from inside.

I pass by the housewives again, hear the nerve-wracking Egyptian music and the drums and the mechanical clapping. I hate that music, hate those housewives, I tell myself, and walk faster. I head up toward the mosque this time, which is more tiring. I'm not going to *salam aleikum* the SOBs sitting across from the mosque. I can't stand them, them or their stories. How come everything's so calm here, as if nothing's happened? How I hate the people here. They live for their next meal and don't think one step ahead. I hate them all, especially the older ones, who've neglected us and let the situation get as bad as it is. Obsequious nobodies. Look at us now. I'm mad at the lot of them. I don't exactly know what's happening, but it must be something much more serious than a terrorist cell or just some intelligence report or warning about a potential suicide bomber who's entered Israel from Qalqilya or Tul-Karm and hidden out in the village. What the hell are they bringing the students home for? How could that tie in with a warning or a terrorist attack? What's going on here damn it?

I check my mobile again, and the result only makes me feel worse. I'll take the car and then see. First I've got to get the car back, though. The entrance to the village is less crowded by now, but there are still dozens of people milling around. The mayor isn't there anymore. He stationed a few of his thugs in strategic spots to keep people from getting close to the barbed wire. There's no more bottleneck and I can get my car out of there. Maybe I ought to go to the town hall first, to check whether they've had any news. The radio is still playing happy music, talking about the economy, rapes, robberies, Palestinian homes that have been demolished and a few terrorists who've been killed.

I check my wallet and decide I'd better go see my older brother at the bank on my way home, to withdraw a few hundred shekels. The bank is crowded now, because everyone who works outside of the village has decided to use this day off for errands. Luckily for me, I don't have to stand in line. I head straight for the office where my brother works. "Say," my brother greets me, "this is serious, isn't it? People have been coming in and saying that the village is surrounded. What do they say in your paper?" only to discover that I have no way of being in touch with my paper. He goes on, "Must be some very red alerts, targeted alerts," jargon that's become second nature to Arabs living in Israel, thanks to the media, who tend to classify the warnings by their level of severity: general, hot, focused, targeted …

Everyone at the bank is discussing today's events. Nobody's in a hurry to use terms like *closure* or *curfew*. They prefer to wonder what it all means and why soldiers would be surrounding the village. Nothing like this has happened since the beginning of military rule. We've had the occasional roadblock and cars are often checked, but never—not even in the days of the Gulf War or the first Intifada—was there a decision not to let the inhabitants out. The customers at the bank don't seem too rattled. Looks like when all is said and done they accept the decision.

They're upset to be losing a day of work, but they don't see the events as a blatant breach of normal relations between citizens and their country.

I try to look calm too as I answer the questions they and the clerks fling at me. "What do you think, must be a serious terrorist roaming around here, huh?"

"I suppose," I say. And one customer protests, "Shame on you, calling them terrorists. Say *istish'hadi*, say *fida'i*. What's become of us? Are we going to start calling them terrorists too?"

A clerk with rectangular glasses and an official black suit, complete with white kerchief, says, "As far as I'm concerned, they can blow up wherever they want, but what right do they have to hide out here? Don't we have enough problems already? They should just leave us alone. We don't need to take part in this war." Another woman standing in the line that's cordoned off with colored chains says, "The problem is the children. What'll happen if he hides his explosives in the bushes, God forbid, and the children play there and touch them by accident? Those *Daffawiyya* West Bank residents have no shame." The customers burst out laughing. Somehow it was enough for them to hear that word, *Daffawiyya*, to start laughing. Of course people around here felt sorry for them when we saw them on TV, being shot at or trying to stage a protest. That wasn't it at all. Most of the locals identified with the Palestinians on TV, but it's as if the ones on TV were completely different people, not the same as the ones around here who loiter, looking for work. Those weren't Palestinians but just workers who make trouble. No chance any of them would ever be on TV. People in our village identify with pictures from far away, forgetting that those pictures were taken a two minutes' drive away from here.

I don't have the patience for their arguments anymore, I'm really not interested. I know the situation is bad enough even without a Palestinian Intifada or the Israeli occupation or some suicide bomber hiding out in our village. Things are bad in any case. For us, for the Palestinians, it doesn't make any difference. We'll always have wars in this godforsaken place. Take any six feet in this place and you'll find too much damage, too much turmoil, too much chaos in every part of our lives, which means the wars will never end. The real wars in this village are the wars over honor, over power, over inheritances and over parking places. Actually I sometimes think it would be a good idea if war did break out, to distract the inhabitants from their cruel and never-ending little fights. To me it doesn't matter anymore so long as they stay away from me, so long as nobody comes to me when the next disagreement breaks out.

I go into my brother's office and close the door behind me. "So, have things calmed down?" my brother asks. I nod. "Yes, I think things are going to work out. I just overreacted, sorry I scared you."

"No, it really is serious. But what could actually happen?"

"I don't know."

I was debating whether to tell him they'd brought our younger brother home from the dorms in the middle of the night, and not just him, but all of the Arab students at the university. I decide not to because he's liable to tell the others, and we shouldn't create panic for now. I ask my brother for a little money. "A few hundred shekels," I say, "maybe even a thousand if I may."

"You may," my brother says. "There are no ATMs, everything's being done manually, so nobody will know you're overdrawn. Strange, your salary hasn't come in this month."

"I know," I mutter. "There was a problem with the accounting because of this new job they gave me. It should have been in my account by now."

"Lucky for you that you came now," my older brother says. "All hell will break loose here today. The money hasn't come in from the main branch. They wouldn't let the armored car into the village, despite the security escort. And it's Sunday, so the safe is almost empty. Mark my words, unless the money arrives, pretty soon we won't have enough to give people." He's laughing now. "They'll kill us. I told the manager I didn't care. I was getting out of here. I don't have what it takes to fight with these people."

"Listen," I tell him before leaving. "When you get off, come over to Mother and Father's house. There's something I need to talk to you about."

"See you there."

7

Now I know I'm overreacting. I get into the car and immediately turn on the radio. The news will be on in a minute. I drive around, deciding not to go back home yet. The news is all about red alerts coming from the Arab villages and towns. The announcer says that security sources are trying to persuade the government to declare a nationwide state of emergency. The tone is the usual one of the news reporters, and it sounds like something that would hardly be noticed in normal times. But today it's different, it's obvious something's going on. Maybe Israel is planning another large-scale attack on the West Bank. Maybe they've decided to get rid of Arafat and they don't want any clashes with the Arabs within Israel, some of whom are bound to take to the streets. They don't want to have to deal with us on top of everything else. Maybe they're just trying to take preventive measures. And maybe that's really why they sent the Arab students home. Maybe the security people were worried about campus demonstrations and decided to make sure it didn't happen, to prevent clashes between Arab and Jewish students. There are all those studies now about the Arab students, dubbed the "proud generation" because they have the audacity to stand there with flags on Naqbah Day or on Land Day. I try to convince myself that everything's going to be okay, but it doesn't work. They sent in the tanks damn it, so maybe it's not going to blow over as soon as people think. Maybe something big really is happening in this area. It wouldn't do me any harm to stock up on things, would it? I'll tell my wife I had the day off and say I didn't know what to do with the time on my hands, so I decided to do the shopping. I'll say I had no idea what we had in the house, so I bought a bit of everything.

I'll do my best not to arouse the suspicion of the salespeople. A shopping spree might create the wrong impression on a day like this. People might think that as a journalist I know something that shows we ought to be getting ready for something big. They might get the idea that I have some secret information about a war that's about to break out in the region. I decide to make the rounds of the different grocery stores and to buy a little bit in each one. I'll start with the ones in the more distant neighborhoods, where I don't usually shop. I cruise the streets and stop at the entrance to the first one I see. There's an older woman standing there, someone I've never seen. That's good, because it must mean she doesn't know me either. A bag of flour is the first thing that occurs to me. That's what you buy when you're stocking up, isn't it?

I take one and pay for it, say thank you and proceed to the next grocery store. "Hello," I say with a smile, trying to seem as natural as possible. I ask the salesman for another bag of flour. If he has one of the big ones, a fifty-kilo bag, that would be great. He does. I pay for it and move on to the next store. "Could I have a bag of rice, please?" I take it, say thank you and move on. All of the stores are running low on dairy products. The trucks from Tnuva Dairies and all the other dairies haven't been able to make the morning delivery because of the roadblocks. I take a few liters of milk, two packages of cheese, some banana yogurt for the baby and a few bottles of my wife's favorite soft drink. In the pharmacy, I take all but one of the cans of formula for one-year-olds. By the time I get to the stores in my own neighborhood, the trunk and both seats are piled high with groceries. I stop at the one nearest my home, smile, greet the owner, who is one of our neighbors, and ask for nothing but a pack of American cigarettes. He asks if they've removed the roadblocks yet, and I shrug as if it's no concern of mine.

8

I'll pick up my wife at school today. I've got time. First I'll unload all the groceries from the car. I'd rather she didn't see the bags of flour and rice. I'll cram them into the little room that we use for storage. I pile the dairy products into the fridge, and feel I've overdone it a bit. We'll pass the expiration date before we use them all up. We hardly eat at home damn it. We usually skip breakfast, so we won't even get to the dairy things. I put the canned goods and the formula in the kitchen cabinets and feel bad about spending money I don't even have. Fuck, if the ATMs were working, even my brother couldn't help me withdraw money from my account. It used to be so convenient to be able to pick up the phone and find out if your salary had been deposited in your account yet and what the balance was, but now it seems like a nightmare. He'll realize soon enough that the paper is hardly paying me anything. I shouldn't have lied to him about the problem with the accounting department. Damn it, I can't go on lying this way. I've got to transfer my account to a different branch, one in the city, maybe. I'll say it's closer to work and that I spend most of my day there anyway, so it'll be easier for me to get to my branch directly from work. It shouldn't be too complicated to transfer an account from one branch to another. It's not as if I'm changing banks. I hope you don't need to close an account before you can move it to a different branch, I mean I hope it doesn't actually have to be in the black. Not that I owe the bank very much, but I don't have even a small amount in my account right now. I can't believe I've spent almost all of the thousand shekels today to stock up for a war that won't happen. Everything's probably blown over by now, I tell myself and go check if the phone's working yet. It isn't.

The doorbell rings as I'm about to leave. A twelve-year-old boy is standing in the entrance with some tissues, some lighters and a picture of the al-Aqsa Mosque. "Special for you, sir, tissues for two shekels, a lighter for half a shekel, ten for four. Have some, and may Allah protect your children, sir." I look at him, standing there and begging, with tears in his eyes. I try not to pity him, to remember what Ashraf told me about the hundred-shekels minimum that those bastards make each day thanks to their knack for making us feel sorry for them. I remind myself that I don't have money to spare and that if I buy from him even once, he'll be back at this address every time. "Sorry, I don't need any," I say. And he goes on begging, with his eyes all moist. "Please, sir, for my parents, and may God bless you and your family, may God bless your relatives who've died, please, sir, take something." I shake my head and lock the door, trying to block out the voice of the boy who runs after me as I get into my car and drive off. I feel a pang in my chest.

It's the first time I've picked up my wife from work. I mean, the first time since we got back. Before that, I'd pick her up almost every day. The paper wasn't far from the school where she taught and I didn't want her taking buses. Here she can manage. She could even come home on foot. It's not far at all. It's almost one-thirty, and they're about to finish the sixth period.

My wife teaches in the same school where I used to go. She went there too, but a few years after me. Some kids are playing ball in the yard. Their teacher is sitting on a chair under one of the trees that kids in my class planted on *Tu b'Shvat,* Israeli Arbor Day. The teacher's gaze alternates between the kids and her watch. I go upstairs and start walking down the long hallway past the classrooms. I look inside as I pass, in search of the one where my wife is teaching. I can hear the Hebrew lessons and the kids echoing the teacher as loud as they can, *"abba"* (father), *"imma"* (mother). Third grade, I tell myself, that's when they start learning Hebrew. Every now and then I nod in the direction of one of the teachers who taught me, or someone I met at our house when a group of teachers came to welcome my wife after we moved back. Ustaz Walid, the history teacher, sees me, interrupts his lesson and invites me into his classroom. He shakes my hand and declares to the students, "He was like you once, one of my students. But he did all his homework, he was a good student, and look where he is now. He's a distinguished journalist, who appears on TV. And you don't want to wind up as factory workers, you want to get to the university too, right?" To which the whole class replies at the top of their voices, "Yes, Mr. Walid."

I nod, and don't know where to hide, I'm so embarrassed. What he says is even slightly painful. I know that journalism was a last resort for me because my score on the psychometric exam prevented me from applying to medical school or law school. Besides, my days as a distinguished journalist are slowly drawing to an end, so that even when I do find a good story that I don't even have to struggle for, a story that's happening to me damn it, in my own village, I can't pick up the phone and talk to my editor.

My wife seems taken aback to see me in the hallway. I smile at her, to make sure she knows there's nothing wrong. She leaves her class for a minute. "Anything wrong? Why aren't you at work?"

"There's some kind of roadblock at the entrance to the village."

"Yes, I heard something about that, but I thought you must have made it out before they closed the road."

"I didn't, even though I've got loads of work, but it's no big deal. You're about to finish, right?"

"In a minute. Come on in."

I go into her classroom. The children are giggling, whispering to one another. Grade 4-a, the same classroom I was in. My wife gives them homework for the following lesson. All of the questions, I to 6, in the chapter about the *halutzim*, the Jewish pioneers. My wife is a geography teacher, and they're still teaching the same material they taught twenty or thirty years ago. She writes the words on the blackboard— *swamps, eucalyptus trees, malaria, diseases, mosquitoes, children dying, sand, desert.*

I doubt the children know who those *halutzim* were. I had never understood they were Jewish immigrants. It was never stated in so many words. I was convinced they were wise heroes that all of us ought to admire because they invented important things like netting for windows and doors, to keep out the poisonous mosquitoes which used to kill babies.

Sometimes I wonder if my wife herself knows that the pioneers were Jewish immigrants. Sometimes, when I look at the tests she's correcting, I wonder if she knows what the Jewish National Fund is, considering she's been singing its praises for years. My guess is that she hasn't a clue. She just accepts what the books say at face value. She's always been a good girl, a good wife. If the JNF spends money on land, public parks and playgrounds, that's what she'll tell her students.

My wife doesn't give much thought to questions like that. She's never really had a chance to know the world outside the village. She's all of twenty-three. Soon as she graduated from high school she entered Beit Berl Teachers College, like all the good girls do. The best thing a girl can do is become a teacher. Girls who attend Beit Berl succeed in retaining their honor despite going to school. The college is very close to the village. They go there each morning and return home in the afternoon. Unlike women who go to a university, they don't have to stay away from home, and everyone knows what bed they slept in. The Beit Berl girls are considered the best match. They're in high demand. You could say they're both well educated and respectable, besides which they find convenient jobs, which allow them to get home early and to be on vacation precisely when their children are. That's more or less what my parents explained to me about my future wife before they went to ask her parents for her hand. "There's nothing better than marrying a teacher," my mother said, and she still says so.

I doubt my wife knows who Berl Katznelson was, the man that Beit Berl College is named after. In fact, I'm pretty sure she thinks he was a hero and an exemplary educator, because that's what it says on the sign at the entrance to the college.

The bell rings. They've replaced the large copper bell, the one the principal used to operate with an iron rod. They have an electric bell now, one that plays a catchy theme song from a famous movie. The children are delighted. They pick up their chairs and put them on their desks, then rush out of the classroom. My wife packs her bag and is the last to leave. The children emerge from school, running. Some of them stop at the kiosk near the front gate, jostling and buying grape-flavored ice pops.

"So what'll you do?" my wife asks. "Won't you go to work today?"

"No," I say, and I understand she thinks the roadblock was only put there for the morning and that things are back to normal. I look at her now, among her students, and suddenly she seems so small, so young. We've had some nice moments, I think. We have. I'm sure of it. I march down the school hallways with her. A few other teachers wave to us. I know they're watching us. I wonder what they think. I'm sure their thoughts about us are good ones. It crosses my mind that to an outside observer we must seem like the perfect couple, who've done everything by the unwritten book of the village. For some reason, this thought gives me new hope. Why not, in fact? What, just because of money? Someday soon things will all work out. I know they will. I walk out of my elementary school with a little smile on my lips.

9

As always, we're eating supper at my parents'. It's been almost two months since we moved here, and we still haven't cooked so much as a single meal. My wife and my older brother's wife are sitting in the kitchen talking about the schools where they work. My older brother's wife is a teacher too. She teaches science in junior high. They've known one another since their college days. My three-year-old nephew is chasing a ball from the kitchen into the living room. Every few minutes he screams, "Goal," and my brother cheers. My mother's in the living room, holding my daughter in her arms and rocking her to sleep. My father's in his customary spot on the sofa, looking preoccupied, a bit more than usual, scratching his palms and waiting for another newscast. In Hebrew this time.

There isn't much to do in this village except sit around with one of our families, mine or my wife's. Actually, the two houses we were born in, my wife and I, have become the two focal points of our lives. And we're not the only ones. Everyone here is like that. The life of my older brother and his wife, for instance, revolves around the homes of his in-laws and our parents, even though they tend to cook at their own home from time to time and to have dinner on their own too. Whenever they do, it upsets my mother. "I don't mind that she cooks," she says. "Every woman likes to feed her husband, but why don't they let me know? What am I supposed to do with all the food I cooked? Isn't it a shame to let it go to waste?"

My wife prefers to eat at her parents' house. She says she feels more comfortable eating there, and she doesn't get the feeling that someone is watching her the way she does at my mother's.

Even though I enjoy my brother-in-law's company, and even though he's really the only person outside of my immediate family that I talk to in this village, I don't feel comfortable staying for too long at my wife's parents' place. Certainly not now, certainly not when my wife is mad at me, and the devil knows what she's been saying about me to her mother, who generally looks like she resents me and makes me feel I'm the reason for her daughter's unhappiness. I suppose it's true, but I can always claim that the reverse is true too, except I would never complain and I would always take what I have coming to me without trying to change things or improve them. And when it comes to my relations with my wife, I'd say I'm a believer.

My wife constantly blames me for the fact that we've returned to this stifling, bleak village that has nothing to offer her. She mentions my brother and his wife, who take their son from time to time and head for a shopping mall in one of the nearby cities. We go sometimes too, even though I've never figured out why people enjoy spending time at shopping centers, and I've never understood the smile on my wife's face as she strolls through the shops and along the food court, even if she's not about to buy anything.

Every time one of her friends or relatives goes abroad, she goes into mourning, and I'm the object of her litany about how I stole her dream of traveling to a different city, a different country. I've stolen her dream of big hotels and even bigger shopping malls. We've never taken an airplane, we've never left the country. I've always said we don't have enough money to pay for such a trip, and that's the truth, even though it's not what my wife would like to hear. I've never felt I needed those trips. Never gave it a second thought. On the contrary, I find it hard to picture what it is that makes them enjoyable. For some reason, as far as I'm concerned, leaving the country is something I could only do in one direction. I mean, when I think of a plane and of another country, I think of it only as a way of emigrating, of escaping, of deciding never to return here—not ever, not even for a visit.

True, there isn't much to do here even if you'd like to. Unlike the city, which offers lots of stimuli even though I hardly ever feel like doing anything there either. And yet, I don't feel more bored here, and I don't get the urge to do more than what the village routine has to offer someone like me—hanging out in your parents' living room.

There are several cafés in the village, all for men. But generally the men there are much older than me and they pass the time playing cards and *tawlah*. I don't like those games, to tell the truth. I've even managed to forget the rules, which I learned from my father long ago. My father sits in cafés every day. Every afternoon he dresses up, as if he's been invited to an official event, and heads for the café where he's been a regular for decades. He plays with his usual partners, the same three teachers he's been playing against for as long as I can remember. He spends his afternoons there, coming home in time for evening prayers. My brother-in-law Ashraf told me there's a place called the Purple Butterfly too, at the outskirts of the village where you can order alcoholic beverages. Ashraf burst out laughing when I suggested that we go have a drink there. He said the only people who ever went there were the heavy drinkers that everyone in the village knows. "What's gotten into you?" He laughed. "Are you nuts? D'you want to come home with an eye and a foot missing, and be ostracized by your family?"

According to Ashraf's stories, some people from the Islamic Movement had tried to set fire to the Purple Butterfly a few times. In fact they actually did burn it down once, and the owner had insisted on rebuilding it. The pub is holding on, and continues to be the only place in the village where they sell alcohol—thanks to the protection of a gang that charges the owner a monthly fee, not to mention a free run of the bar for the gang members. "They deserve a place where they can have a drink too, don't they?" Ashraf says, and laughs, the way he always does when he tells me those stories. "Something close to home that could get them through withdrawal without their having to go all the way to Tel Aviv for a swig of arrack."

Apart from driving through the streets with radios blaring full blast, the favorite pastime of people around here is weddings. In summer, weddings are an alternative to discotheques. That's where bachelors can fan their tails and do their mating dances, that's where they can really let go and sweat, and stomp their feet for hours on end. The weddings provide another setting, another arena for the machismo match. Bachelors like Ashraf spend almost every summer evening at weddings. He told me that he and some of his friends used to go to Tel Aviv regularly and try their luck at the dance clubs they'd read about in the papers or heard about from the other students, except they never got past the bouncer and had to make do with spending yet another night at one of the dives that admitted just about anyone. "We'd go into places that you wouldn't believe. You'd have the feeling a murder was just waiting to happen, someone was about to waste an enemy or something," he chuckled. "There's nothing like weddings. It's the best bet. Trouble is that if you wind up at an Islamic wedding, you're done for. Sure, everyone's a Muslim, and everyone's becoming religious lately, but I'm talking about the ones who decide that instead of a wedding with music and dancing they'll invite a sheikh to read verses from the Koran and a religion teacher to lecture about the shocking behavior of today's young people at the promiscuous weddings taking place right here in our own village. Lots of people are into that nowadays, and you can't tell anymore what to expect. Sometimes we have to do three weddings in a single evening before we find one without a sheikh."

True, there isn't much to do around here, least of all for someone like me. I don't go to the mosque, I try to stay away from weddings, I don't play cards with men my father's age and I have no desire to visit the only club in the village. But I'm not bored. I mean, I haven't been particularly bored since I moved here. On the contrary, I suffered more before. I don't even miss the nights when we'd go out to look for kicks. At least I've been spared those embarrassing moments, those moments of drunkenness when I could find no rest for my soul. I've been spared the mornings after the nights of drinking, when I felt miserable for not being able to keep my thoughts to myself the night before.

10

"Sh ... sh ... sh ..." my father mutters. The main newscast on Israel TV is beginning. I hate watching the news on Israeli national television. Tanks appear on the screen, and planes and fire are everywhere, and in the background they're playing a military march heralding a war that is about to break out any minute. Everyone is sitting around in silence. My younger brother interrupts his studying and comes out of his room to watch the news. He's got an exam in two days.

They don't mention the words *closure* or *roadblocks*. Instead, there's talk of red alerts or of backup forces being brought into the area of the Arab villages in the Triangle area on the West Bank border. The West Bank has actually been peaceful today, and the Israeli and Palestinian negotiators are continuing with their meetings in Jerusalem. The announcer starts with the economic crisis and the heat wave sweeping over the country, then moves on to the news in full.

Something's wrong. They haven't even shown any tanks or fences. All they talk about are alerts—and they're talking so naturally, as if they're something that's been in the news for two years running. The chief of police for this region arrives in the studio and makes no mention of the new situation. He speaks of Israeli Arabs who have helped the Hamas. Again there's talk of the security risk, and the growing extremism of Israeli Arabs. The finger is pointed toward the leadership, the Islamic Movement. Nothing out of the ordinary.

"Maybe it's a secret operation," my father says. And my younger brother answers, laughing, "How secret could it be when the whole village knows about it? If they'd wanted to surprise someone, they could have come in and arrested him quietly. Is this what you'd call secret?"

Father says they're bound to enter the village tonight and arrest the ones they're after. "'Cause there's no way you can keep anything hidden in this village. Nobody gives a damn and everyone cooperates with the police and the security forces. It stopped being considered betrayal long ago. So if there's anything going on, the General Security Service is bound to know all about it—where and when and how. I'm telling you, they're about to send in one of their select units, and two jeeps, maybe, in the middle of the night. They'll pull it off and leave as if nothing's happened."

"They're just on our case," my older brother says. "Could you imagine anyone in this village pulling off a suicide or joining one of the Palestinian organizations? It's never happened, has it?"

Another senior security official appears on the screen, his face disguised to conceal his identity, to talk about the role of Israeli Arabs in terrorist attacks on Jews. He says they're much more dangerous than the Palestinians themselves, because they're more familiar with the Jewish cities and liable to cause greater damage. The same senior official notes that the agenda of today's meeting with the minister of defense included a discussion of the need to announce a state of national emergency.

Just what do they mean?

Then they put on the water commissioner, who announces that the good rainfall of recent months has not eliminated the national water shortage. The Water Council is weighing the possibility of declaring a state of emergency in the water supply.

Something's wrong. I can tell. I know the Israeli media. A closure on an Arab village, and according to my younger brother he's not the only student who was sent home, all the Arab students were sent home from the university; so it stands to reason the Israelis have surrounded some other Arab villages too, if not all of them. I know it's the kind of story the media wouldn't pass up. I know the government must have issued a gag order.

My father says that every time there's been a war, Israel has surrounded the Arab towns and villages within its borders and kept watch on them. But usually it was the Border Police and the regular police who did the job. They never used the army—or tanks damn it—the way they're doing now. My father says maybe the Americans have thrown Israel some important information about an operation—in Syria, maybe—and Israel wants to make sure that life inside the country remains calm. As if anyone else is going to do anything. As if any one of us would ever do anything. Very soon, when they realize we haven't done anything wrong, they'll get out, the way they always do.

My daughter is already asleep. My younger brother goes back to his studies. He says he might as well study because the closure is going to continue and they'll have to give the Arab students a special makeup exam. I carefully lift my daughter out of my mother's arms, and she says that even though it's warm I ought to cover her head on my way home because she's perspiring and is liable to catch cold. My older brother gets up too and calls his son. We walk out of our parents' house. The air outside is completely still. It's stifling. Some guys continue driving up and down aimlessly, keeping their loudspeakers at full volume. Why are they doing it damn it? A series of loud explosions takes my breath away for a moment but I soon realize it's just a wedding. I've got to get a grip.

I tuck the baby into her crib. My wife gets into bed and asks if I'm coming. "Pretty soon," I say, and go up on the roof for a cigarette. I can hear the music from the wedding hall. I study the fields to the north and see the bluish lights of the army jeeps. Every now and then, when the wedding music fades out, you can hear the engines of the tanks. They never turn them off.

PART THREE

*The Paper Didn't Arrive
This Morning Either*

1

She's waking up now, on the morning of the second day that the village has been blocked off. Very slowly, she picks herself up and sits on the right side of the bed, her side. I can feel her yawning, rubbing her eyes and stretching her arms. She doesn't know I'm already awake, or that I didn't sleep a wink all night. She gets out of bed and goes into the bathroom. I hear her turn on the light. She won't shut the door behind her. She's never closed a bathroom door in her life. I hear the familiar trickle and the paper being torn and the wiping. I've always hated listening to her flushing the toilet and pulling her panties back up. Sometimes I think she deliberately tugs at the rubber band around her waist and lets it make a loud sound just to annoy me.

She brushes her teeth. It takes her exactly three minutes. She looks at her watch before starting. That's what the dentist told her ten years ago, and ever since then she's made a point of it, morning and evening. Three minutes on the dot, not a second more or less, with the same motions the dentists taught them in those special lectures long ago.

She doesn't like using water left in the kettle from yesterday. She pours it out in the kitchen sink, turns on the faucet, refills the kettle and puts it on to boil. She tries starting the flame with the long lighter a few times, and I can picture her pulling her hand away quickly with each attempt. Finally I hear the flame. Now she heads for the baby's room. First she'll pull up the blinds. The baby will wake with a start, try to open her eyes but finding the light too painful she'll blink and put her hands over them. I can hear her say, "Good morning, sweetheart, good morning, good morning," trying to sing it. And the baby groans again, as if she's about to cry, but holds back. Gradually, she'll wake up, in her crib. She'll fall back on the blanket, she'll try to sit up, then she'll fall back again and turn her head to the right and to the left, and finally she'll stand up in bed, holding on to the high wooden railing that keeps her from getting out on her own.

She's coming back into the bedroom now. I lie on my back with my eyes closed. She'll be raising the blinds. She always pulls hard at the cord. It's her way of telling me it's time for me to wake up. I remember how I used to hope she'd find a different way of waking me. With a kiss, maybe, or maybe by stroking my hair, and maybe when I opened my eyes I'd also hear her "Good morning," but those hopes were short-lived. She pulls hard at the aluminum blinds and furiously unleashes the sunlight that blasts me each morning with all its might. She thinks I'm only now waking up. I open my eyes, and I can see her standing over the bed. It must be almost seven. The alarm clock froze a long time ago. Sometimes it springs back to life and its hands suddenly advance by a few notches, only to stop again. Sometimes the second hand tries to climb up, and you can see it struggling to reach the next second, but it can't. It tries for awhile, then gives up and stops short. She doesn't really need an alarm clock anymore and we haven't had to buy a new one. Every morning she's the first to wake up, right on time, and she wakes up the rest of the household.

She's wearing her *dishdash*, the kind all the Arab women wear. A black one with red and green embroidery near the top. I used to hate that *dishdash* and I thought that if she went to bed naked or with any other type of pajamas, a two-piece, maybe, everything would be so different, but she's never parted with her *dishdashes* and there was no chance of her running out of them. Because almost every time her parents visited us, her mother made sure to bring along a new one. When the baby was born and her mother spent a few nights with us I discovered that she sleeps in a *dishdash* too. She crosses her arms, placing her right arm on her left hip and her left arm on her right hip, grabs the edges and, with one quick move, pulls it over her head.

Now she's standing there in nothing but her undies, and I wonder as I watch her undress if I've ever been attracted to her. With one hand she stretches the skin of her back. The other arm is raised to let her look behind her from under her armpit and examine her backside. It's a movement that repeats itself every morning, and I've never been able to figure it out. Why doesn't she use the mirror damn it, just six feet away from the bed? The baby's crying interrupts her movements and she quickly puts on her bra and runs to the baby's room while hooking it with both arms behind her back. "What's the matter, sweetheart? What's wrong? Shhhh," she calls out, and picks up the baby. I can picture her clasping the baby with one arm to the left side of her body, and the baby spreads her legs and encircles her mother's stomach, hanging on to the white bra with both hands.

"Your bottle, you want your bottle, here's your bottle." She pours some warm water from the kettle into the baby's bottle, takes some formula out of an upper cabinet in the kitchen and counts the spoonfuls out loud as if singing to the baby: *"Wahad, tneyn . . ."* checking with her tongue to make sure the milk isn't too warm, handing it to the baby, putting her back in her crib and returning to the bedroom to get dressed.

She pulls her pants up to her knees, then pulls one side up, struggling to get past her wide hips, then the other side. I'm always surprised to see how in the end her pants do close easily over her stomach. She puts on a white blouse I bought her when we were engaged. To tell the truth, I bought something else and took a receipt and she returned what I'd bought and chose a white button-down blouse with a collar shaped like two big triangles, like a butterfly's wings. She pulls her sandals out from under the bed while trying to amuse the baby, and shouts from a distance, "Milk, you're drinking your milk, Mommy's coming, my pretty, you're so pretty." And she blurts out at me as she heads back from the bedroom to the baby's room, "Well, what's up, don't you want any coffee? It's seven-fifteen already."

2

I know the paper didn't arrive this morning either. For a few hours now I've been trying to concentrate, waiting to hear the paper being delivered. Maybe they'll come on a bike, maybe by car. I've been waiting to hear the thud the paper makes as they hurl it at the front door, but I haven't heard it. I go downstairs and try to turn on the TV with the remote, but nothing happens. The red lamp under the screen is turned off. This time I don't even bother checking the fuse box. I know they've cut off our power too.

I can't see the road from my house, but I can hear the commotion. "*Shu sar?* What happened?" the neighbors are shouting from their windows, and the ones walking in the street shout back, "They've killed two people," "They shot at people," and "They must have caught some suicide bombers." I tell my wife to stay home for now, and put on my pants and shirt and go to my parents' place. They're up too by now and are standing in the doorway that faces the street. Mother is clasping her hands together and cursing the Jews, and Father is puffing at his cigarette and saying that people say some workers were shot trying to get across the roadblock. My mother asks me not to leave the house. "What's the point? What can you see out there any-way?" Their neighbor's son, Khalil, who works as a nurse at the hospital in Kfar Sava, is returning in his car. My father signals him to come closer, Khalil parks outside his house and comes toward us in his white jacket. He had thought that if he approached the soldiers in his white jacket, they'd realize he was a nurse who wants to get to work. It's just as well that he didn't cross the roadblock, he says. There was a pickup there with a couple of workers in it. The owner, a contractor, tried to break through the barbed wire with his vehicle and took a tank shell. Just like that, no questions asked. He and the two workers died on the spot, and some of those behind the road-block were hit by shrapnel. The Israelis didn't send an ambu-lance and they wouldn't let them be taken to hospital. The injured were picked up and taken to the infirmary. One of them was in a bad way—what could they do for him at the infir-mary? He needs an operation urgently. The infirmary barely has a thermometer.

"And what's going on now?" Father asks.

"The whole village is out there. The mayor and his cro-nies are asking people to move away and are trying to keep things quiet. The parents of the contractor and of the two workers, one of them from the village and one from the West Bank, are trying to get through with spades and knives, to get back at the soldiers. One worker's father fainted and had to be taken to the infirmary too."

"Maybe now they'll get out to avoid a confrontation with the mob," Father says, and Khalil, in his jacket, explains there's no chance and that, on the contrary, they've been bringing more and more soldiers in, and they're standing there with their pistols and their machine guns and the barrels of the tanks as if they're expecting a war. *"Allah yustur,"* he says. "They're up to something. What are they thinking? And they've cut off the power, to boot. They've gone completely crazy."

3

"It could take time," I tell my parents and my brother. "We've got to get things ready before it's too late, to buy enough food for at least a week."

For some reason, a week seems to me now like the longest that the thing everyone calls a roadblock—and nobody really knows if it's a siege or a closure or the devil knows what—can continue. My father laughs and says I'm overreacting. My mother and my older brother agree with me. My brother says that, who knows, there might be confrontations with the soldiers and they'll declare a closure, looks like they'll stop at nothing now. I tell them they shouldn't buy too many dairy products or too much meat or anything that needs to be refrigerated, because there's no telling when the power will go back on.

My father says we're exaggerating. True, he hasn't come across a tank shell since '48, but it must be a regrettable mistake of some soldier who misinterpreted a command when he saw the pickup coming straight at him and thought it must be a terrorist and a car bomb. Those soldiers have been in the territories and in Lebanon, and all of them are so panicky they can't tell a loyal Arab from an enemy. My father says the soldier will get told off by his commanders in no time. He's convinced that right after the incident they'll be issuing an apology and the soldiers will leave. The power will be back soon too, because if it isn't just an ordinary malfunction it must be that they cut the power because it was much easier for the soldiers to operate in the dark. They've probably finished their mission by now, and if it hadn't been for that idiot contractor with his pickup, everything would have been behind us by now.

My father has full faith in the state, he always has. When we were little, everybody assumed that he'd been appointed supervisor in the Ministry of Education because of his qualifications. He doesn't really have an academic degree, and he barely finished the teachers' seminary in Jaffa. Every now and then I'd get into a fight with students whose parents had told them that my father was in cahoots with the authorities, and I'd always scream at them that they were just jealous, and sometimes I cried when they said he was collaborating with the Jews. Because it wasn't true. He just had a few good friends. Besides, I knew everyone liked him. When we were little, I remember how whole families used to come to see him almost every day with gift-wrapped things, and they'd talk to him very respectfully and ask him to find a job for their children or to fix situations that they couldn't fix themselves. My father was a good person and he helped people, and it had nothing to do with the presents. He always said he didn't want those, and that he only took them because the people insisted.

When I grew up, I realized there was no way an Arab would get a senior appointment in the Ministry of Education if the government didn't have a vested interest in him. It's still that way, in fact. My father says he's never informed on anyone and that all he ever wanted was to help the students. He says he got the job thanks to his good reputation and not because he'd collaborated with the security service. Granted, he doesn't have an academic degree, but we're talking about thirty years ago, and who had an academic degree in those days? Who even got as far as the teachers' seminary in Jaffa? It was true. My father was no collaborator. All he did was vote for the Labor Party and host some parlor meetings in his home. It meant inviting some of the Jews that we used to see on TV to come here and talk, and Father got the whole family to vote like him.

Somehow, something that had once been considered a betrayal became perfectly legitimate in the eighties and nineties. Those were the years when the Arab citizens not only resigned themselves to being citizens of Israel, they even grew to like their citizenship and were worried that it might be taken away from them. They no longer dreamed of being part of the big Arab world stretching "from the ocean to the Gulf" the way they used to. On the contrary, the idea of becoming part of the Arab world even began to frighten them. They truly believed the Israeli politicians who claimed that "relative to the Arab states, the situation of the Israeli Arabs is amazing," a sentence that always shut people up when they started talking about discrimination. People were afraid they wouldn't get their National Insurance allowances anymore, or that a day would come when they'd find themselves in a country without medical insurance, welfare, pensions for widows or single parents or the next of kin, allowances for the elderly and the disabled, unemployment benefits or subsidies.

As soon as the Oslo Accords were signed, my father could take pride in the fact that he'd belonged to the party that had recognized the PLO and was ready to establish a state for the Palestinians. Actually, there was no real difference between the loudmouths who voted for an Arab party and those who supported the left-wing Zionists. Both adopted similar slogans, all about "peace and equality," so what was the problem exactly?

I know some people thought my father had a lot of money, that he'd received huge sums from the state or from his party, especially when Labor was in power, but it isn't true. My father worked hard his whole life, and that's something I know for a fact. He did everything he could to make sure we got a university education, and to be able to build each of us a home someday. I remember how he used to come home from his Ministry of Education job in the afternoon, rest awhile, and then go to work at another job. For years he moonlighted at a frozen-meat factory. In the afternoons he'd head for one of the kibbutzim nearby. Then they'd give him a pickup with a large refrigeration compartment in back, and a freezer full of poultry and sausages and hamburger, all of it frozen. Father would distribute the meat in the Arab villages in the area. He was too embarrassed to work in our own village. I figured it out right away. He never told anybody about that job. Only we, the family, knew about it. Actually, I'm not sure my brothers knew either. I'd insist on doing the rounds with him. At first he refused. "You just see to your studies, and the rest will take care of itself," he always said. Only when he came to accept that it wouldn't hurt my schoolwork—that I'd finished my homework even before he got home from work at his day job—did he agree. "I know," he said, "your teachers are always telling me how well you are doing and that you really should have skipped a grade." That's how I began joining my father every afternoon. I'd watch him put on his big green jacket and walk into the refrigeration room. He'd pull out boxes and pile them up in the back of the pickup, which had a big winking chicken painted over its side. I'd help my father carry the boxes. I was in ninth grade by then, and pretty strong. I loved working with him. It didn't take too long either. Usually we finished making the rounds of all the grocery stores in two to three hours. I soon came to know all the grocery owners in the area. After a while I started carrying the boxes myself. I wouldn't let my father touch them. All he had to do was settle accounts with the grocers while I unloaded the goods. It wasn't hard, not at all.

My father was very happy. In every grocery store he'd tell the owner or whoever was around, "That's my son, the best student in the class, the best student in the whole school." He always smiled as he said it. So my father was no traitor and no collaborator.

Ever since he retired, he's stopped being active in the party. All he does is vote for it in the Knesset elections. After the outbreak of the second Intifada and the events of October 2000, he even stopped trying to persuade us to vote for Labor. Mother voted like him, because she always does whatever he does. I don't know who my older brother voted for, maybe the Islamic

Movement, but I boycotted the elections. It was my own decision, not because the Arab parties said that was what we should do. Sometimes I even hate them and their way of thinking.

My older brother says he'll buy some things at the grocery store now, and he'll finish his chores when he gets home from work. Mother tells Father we have nothing to lose. Whatever food we have we'll eat, and she'll send my brother to the store right away with some money and a shopping list.

4

I go back home. My wife is feeding the baby. "What happened?" she asks.

"Nothing. Some idiot tried to run the roadblock."

"The roadblock? It's still there? You mean you won't be going to work today either?"

"You'd better stay home too."

"What do you mean? I can't. But I only have five classes today. I'll be home early. What will you do all day? How about cleaning up a bit?"

"Yeah, we'll see. But I'd like the baby to stay with me today."

"Great. She'll love it. Won't you, sweetheart? Won't you? You'll stay with Daddy."

In a way I'm happy they've continued the roadblock today too. It sort of saves me from the useless trip to the paper and from aimlessly roaming the streets. On the other hand, what the hell is going on here?

The baby smiles and finishes the whole bottle. My wife hands her over to me and goes to the bathroom. I'm so sorry I have a little girl. What a fool I was to decide to bring a child into the world in a situation like this. It wasn't just the road-block and yesterday's events, but generally it seemed to me really inhumane to bring children into a world like ours in a region like ours. The problem is that my wife got pregnant before the present Intifada broke out. Everything seemed different then, and my own way of thinking was different too. I can even say I was optimistic. My career was going well and relations between Arabs and Jews were beginning to improve. Sometimes I think it all happened because of the baby, as a kind of retribution. Religious people would say God was testing us. I try to smile at the baby, as if to convince her that everything's fine, that she's living in surroundings that are just the way I'd planned for her. When I think about how quickly things deteriorated, it's mind-blowing.

I'd rather the three of us stayed together today. That's how I am when I have a sense that things are dangerous—I like to see all the people that I worry about sticking together, but I don't have the strength to explain to her about how frightened I am and to persuade her to stay home.

We're walking together and she says good-bye to the baby, I tell her to take care of herself, follow her with my eyes till she's out of sight and go into my parents' home with the baby in my arms.

5

My parents are getting dressed to pay a condolence call. My father pays condolence calls every time anyone in the village dies. He and two other adults in the family are regarded as the official condolence callers, and for decades the three of them have paid these calls on the second day of the mourning, after evening prayers. When the death isn't natural, or when the deceased is someone important, or when a friend or someone young dies in his prime, the three relatives modify their standard procedure and don't wait for the second day but try to make it to the funeral as well. My mother wears a kerchief and attends too. When they reach the road, they split up—Mother joins the women and Father walks along with the men. Many men and women are walking toward the house, trying to keep quiet, speaking in a whisper, the men walking on the right side of the road and the women on the left. I feel kind of sorry that I can't join the funeral procession, which is bound to set out from the homes of the parents—the contractor's and the workers'—toward the mosque, and from there to the cemetery. Too bad I offered to take the baby, because it could certainly have added some human interest to the story I'll write for the paper. I'm still convinced I'll be covering the whole chain of events once the roadblock is removed. If the closure is lifted tomorrow, I may still get the story written in time for this weekend's supplement.

When my mother gets back, I'll give her the baby and go out to see what's happening, how people are taking it. My younger brother is back home, holding two plastic bags so heavy he can barely lift them. "Mother's gone crazy," he says, dumping the bags on the kitchen counter. Mostly they're full of canned goods, corn, tuna, pickles, beans, peas, *ful*, chickpeas. He says the store was packed and that he practically had to hit this older woman who tried to get ahead of him. He says there were loads of people there and that some of the things that Mother had ordered were sold out already. He couldn't find any flour, for instance.

My brother takes a seat in the living room, first beside me, stroking the baby's head and smiling at her. She smiles back. Then he sits on the sofa farthest from us, pulls out a pack of cigarettes and lights one. "So, the folks have gone to a funeral?" he asks.

"Yeah. Since when do you smoke?"

"For almost a year. You know how it is at university, don't you?" He smiles and adds in a more serious voice, "What do you say? Should I bother studying? Do you think there's any chance I'll get back to Tel Aviv tomorrow?"

"Sure, you've got to study for the exam."

He takes a puff at his cigarette and tells me that in the beginning, when the security service knocked at his door, he thought they were rounding up the students they considered problematic, the political activists, the ones who showed up at campus rallies. But with him in the police car were students who were so good that they always made a point of keeping out of politics and just focused on their studies. My brother's description takes me by surprise. I have the feeling I hardly know him anymore. I'd never imagined him as a smoker, and now he tells me he's a campus activist. "And in what party are you active?" I ask him.

"I'm with the Communists."

"The Communists? And just how did you wind up with the Communists?"

"Well, you know how it is. You've been, haven't you? You meet people. Your friends are active in the party, so you decide you want to be active too, but it's mainly because of how they treated me. Suddenly I see our problems. Suddenly I understand what it means to be hated, what racism and discrimination are. In the dorms, they make sure you're put into the Arabs' rooms, which are the worst rooms there are. One room for Arabs on each floor, to make sure there aren't too many of us in any one place, to keep us in a minority status even on the floor. You know how there's a single refrigerator for each two rooms? Well, the day I got there, I went into the kitchen to get a compartment for myself and my roommate from Djat, and this Jewish guy asked if I'd share a compartment with him. He said it was lucky I'd come because he was so worried he'd wind up having to share with an Arab."

With my younger brother it's hard to tell what he is, especially with his ponytail and his hard-rock clothes. Like most of the young people who join the Communist Party, my brother doesn't know the first thing about Communism. They know it's a party that aims at equality between Jews and Arabs, between the poor and the rich, but they haven't a clue about its principles. We continue talking and I try to find out more about his Communism. I discover he knows who Lenin was but he's never heard of Trotsky. He can curse the capitalists but knows nothing about the concept of a proletariat or the distribution of capital. The Communist slogans suited him, there were a few guys there from the law faculty where he studies, and that's why he chose the Communists. He adds that there are some really cool Christian girls from the Galilee there too, not afraid to smoke in front of everyone, dressing right and joining the guys for a beer. It's not that my younger brother is dumb. Not at all. He's smart, and someday he'll learn to tell the difference between them all. I don't think I understood much about the different parties at his age either, or just what the conflict is all about. My brother asks me not to say a word to Father, 'cause he'll kill him. Father's motto has always been that if you want to amount to anything and if you want to do well at school, you've got to stay away from politics. Girls and politics. He makes me swear not to mention the cigarettes either, because Father is liable to make him stop school and come back home. I tell him he's exaggerating, but promise not to say anything. My younger brother goes back to his studies, the baby begins to cry.

6

My little girl has fallen asleep and I put her down on my parents' bed, the one they bought on their wedding day more than thirty years ago, the one they still sleep in. I go home, get the car keys and get in the car to listen to the news. The heat is overpowering, and it isn't even noon. The radio dials are boiling. I try to turn them without getting burned, and pull away quickly. They're playing the commercials now, the ones that come right before the news. Advertising air conditioners, savings plans at the bank and special deals on trips abroad or at local resorts. The news begins with an announcement that the government, in cooperation with the army, has decided to declare a general state of emergency. Officials in the security system are talking of the imminent danger of an Arab uprising and about red alerts related to certain people in the Arab sector who are planning to attack Jewish citizens and state institutions. Later, toward the middle of the newscast, they mention our village. The announcer reports an attempt to attack some soldiers who were conducting a routine patrol near the entrance to the village. "An attempted terrorist attack," he says, "which ended without casualties thanks

to our soldiers' alertness." He's referring to the incident with
the contractor and the worker in the pickup. Needless to say,
there's no mention of the Arab casualties, and it stands to reason they don't have the facts anyway. There's no way of com-
municating with people in the village, after all.

The situation has become unbearable. They're up to something, it's obvious by now, and they're laying the foundations
in Jewish public opinion. For two years now, politicians, ministers, members of Knesset and security experts have been talking about a "cancer in the heart of the nation," an "imminent
danger," a "fifth column," and a "demographic problem that
threatens to undermine the Jewish fiber of the state." What do
they expect? What the hell do they expect? The Jewish public
is already filled with hatred and a sense of danger. Just how far
do they expect it to go? I look for the Arabic news on Voice of
Israel. I know it's the government propaganda channel—still,
maybe they'll give some more information—but their frequency
has been cut too.

There's a loud noise coming from the street, and I run
back to see what's happening. My younger brother is standing
outside watching. It's the funeral, judging by the noise, the largest funeral there's ever been in this village. We can't see it, but
the cries of *"Allahu akbar"* reverberate through the village. A
few women come out of their houses all excited and watch
the funeral procession. They must have taken the bodies out
of the mosque by now. My wife returns home and tells me
that the high school kids came to the elementary school, entered each of the classrooms and announced a general strike

and a demonstration. "I hope the younger ones go home and don't get into trouble now, that's all they need," she says.

"I'm glad you're back," I tell her. "The baby's fallen asleep and I'm going out to see what's happening."

"What for? What can you do to help?"

"It's not for me, it's part of my job," I say, and feel the rush of the adrenaline that used to course through my veins when I set out to do a story.

"If things heat up, come back right away, do me a favor. Don't be late, okay?" my wife says, and it reminds me of the days when I used to cover stories on the West Bank and it worried her. How I've missed her worrying.

The cemetery is teeming with people. Everyone is silent, allowing the prayer for the dead to be conducted peacefully. As soon as it's over, the crowd cries out, *"Allahu akbar,"* and continues walking. Almost nobody goes home after the burial. The funeral has turned into a demonstration, possibly the largest the village has ever seen. A village that kept out of trouble even on Land Day and in the October events because it knew where its interests lay. The demonstration is being led by high school students repeating slogans they've heard from the Palestinians on TV. "With blood and might we shall redeem you, *ya shahid.*" They'd decided that the contractor and his two workers were *shahids.* The students march toward the council building. Some climb up on the roof, pull down the Israeli flag and burn it. The demonstrators whistle and boo and call out slogans against the State of Israel and against the prime minister—Swine, the Murderous Dog.

Very soon activists from the Islamic Movement join in, equipped with a pickup with loudspeakers and green party flags. Mostly they're thinking of the political capital they can get out of it, and so are the Communists, who are waving red flags and singing their slogans and calling out the names of their leaders. The pan-Arabists are not far behind, with their yellow banners and the pictures of their leader stuck onto construction-paper placards. They all join a single procession at first, and call out the same slogans against the army and in support of the *shahids*. Very slowly the groups drift apart. The Islamic Movement activists lead the way, followed by the pan-Arabists, then the Communists, each group shouting different slogans, and then come the masses of demonstrators, ordinary people who've come for the funeral and decided to join in, to unleash their anger, show their solidarity and maybe do something to alleviate the grief of the bereaved families.

The demonstrators are marching through the village, and people keep joining them. Women take their place at the end of the procession, careful not to come too close to the men. The more neighborhoods they go through, the more demonstrators there are. Their faces are more angry than concerned. The shops, the offices and the restaurants close as a sign of mourning. It isn't a strike. The demonstrators are making their way toward the exit from the village, toward the roadblock. I take my place in the rear, as close to the women as possible. I'm not taking any chances. If they fired this morning, they might fire now too.

The mayor and a large group of his young relatives are there, with their backs to the barbed-wire fence, waiting for the demonstrators, signaling them from a distance not to go any closer to the makeshift fence. The mayor hasn't a chance of keeping them away. If the demonstrators were inclined to come closer, he couldn't stop them. It just hasn't occurred to them. Nobody's willing to run the risk, and the procession draws to a halt at the roadblock. The demonstrators are shouting their tried and true slogans into their megaphones. The Muslims are shouting *"Allahu akbar,"* and *"Khaybar khaybar, ya Yahud,"* and that the Army of Muhammad will soon be back. The Communists are singing songs of solidarity and support of the Communist Youth Movement and the pan-Arabists are praising Nasser. Gradually the demonstrators begin to disperse, and soon there is nobody left facing the roadblock. In the distance, the soldiers can be seen getting up and putting down their weapons.

7

The atmosphere in the village has changed. More and more people are worried. The grocery stores, the bakeries and the restaurants that reopened after the demonstration have never seen so many shoppers. The stores were more crowded than on a Saturday before the Intifada, when Jews used to arrive from all around Israel.

There are one or two grocery stores in each neighborhood, a total of fifteen in the village as a whole. At the entrance, very close to the roadblocks, are the larger stores, for people arriving from the outside. The owners of those outlets used to be considered very lucky. Many Jews preferred shopping in the village, because they were sure the Arabs charged less, which wasn't really true. The fact is that most of the villagers actually shopped in the city and saved quite a bit.

Despite the heat wave, the streets are full of kids and teenagers standing around in groups and talking about the demonstration, about the casualties, the soldiers and the roadblock. Everyone is convinced that Israel is about to drop an atom bomb on Iraq or Iran. Some of the youngsters are even swearing that they heard it on broadcasts from the Arab states. They're saying that American and Israeli forces have launched an all-out offensive against the Arab world, and they're afraid that we, the Israeli Arabs, will undermine their efforts by photographing targets for the Iraqis. Others swear they heard the Egyptian army has conquered Beersheba by now and is quickly advancing toward Tel Aviv, and that the Israelis have decided to hold us hostage.

Men and women are marching down the road, perspiring and carrying home large bags of food. As for me, I seek out the least busy-looking grocery so I can buy candles, batteries and maybe another pack of cigarettes. I've figured out that the food I bought can feed the whole family for at least a week, so that even if my older brother doesn't manage to buy everything on our mother's list, we'll be okay. The thought that I've saved my family, so to speak, gives me a sense of victory. I quickly curb the feeling.

The older people who normally spend all their time at the entrance to the mosque aren't there. They've taken their seats in the mourners' tent. Two neighbors are standing in the doorways of their homes talking about an episode in an Egyptian series that was on TV last night. One of them says she doesn't know what she'll do if the power doesn't come back on by nightfall. She'll go crazy if she misses the next episode. I know the series they're talking about. My wife has become addicted to it too and I myself try not to miss the story of the textile merchant who was once poor and has turned into one of the richest men in Cairo. He takes four wives. Three of them get along well, but the fourth is a wicked woman who is only after his money. Slowly I make my way home, and decide to enter the neighborhood grocery store despite the crowd inside.

A bunch of women are standing in line to pay. Some of them have come from other neighborhoods. The shelves of canned goods have been swept clean. There are no bags of rice or flour left either. One of the neighbors comes into the shop and screams at the owner to bring out the merchandise he has in his storerooms. The owner swears that he doesn't even have any left for himself. He'd meant to keep a bag of rice for himself, but it's all gone. He swears by all that's holy. The neighbor gets even more annoyed and looks at the strange women standing in line and goes on screaming at the owner that he shouldn't be selling to strangers, that he should be responsible enough to keep his merchandise for his regular customers, the people in his own neighborhood, his faithful clientele.

Practically the only things left in the grocery store are candy, snack bars and condiments. The furious neighbor, sporting a hat with the logo of a local transportation company, makes the rounds of the grocery, wringing his hands and saying, "What's the matter with everyone? Have people gone crazy or what?" and then leaves.

They've hardly touched the candles or the batteries. I take two packages of each and get in line. The owner recognizes me and signals that I can leave. He knows I'll be back to pay later. On my way out I ask if there are any cigarettes left. He bends over and pulls out two packs of a local brand from under the table. "They're the last ones, want them?" The woman facing him is holding a few bills in her hand. She looks in my direction and lets out a hiss that makes me feel uneasy. I say yes, take the two packs and get out of there.

The whole family is at my parents' house. They're outside this time, seeking comfort in the shade of one of the few trees in the yard. "Look at him," Mother says. "He thinks of everything. Who else thought of buying candles?" My father laughs at me for buying so many batteries. "What do you think, that we'll never have electricity again?" Everyone's laughing now. Even my nephew, who doesn't understand any of this, manages a smile. My wife has already told them about my shopping spree yesterday, which she discovered when she went into the storage room.

"So?" Father says. "I see you've decided it's going to be a long war."

My older brother comes to my rescue and tells us that he's hardly managed to buy anything. "And what if things go on this way? Nobody really knows what's happening, so I'm glad you did what you did," he tells me.

My mother goes into the house and returns with a bowl of potatoes and two peelers. I say at once, "Mother, why waste the potatoes? The things in the fridge are about to spoil. Let's eat those first."

Father laughs out loud and coughs. "Yes, the potatoes should be kept for the tough times of the war. By tomorrow we'll have nothing to eat, after all," and he continues coughing.

My wife says I'm right. It really would be a waste. They're going to be cooking all the meat in the three families' freezers today, so there's no need for potatoes. My mother puts them back and says in a ceremonious voice that we have so much meat we won't be needing bread today either. I go inside, enter my parents' bedroom and look for the battery-operated radio. It's the one we used during the Gulf War, when all of us moved into the sealed room at night. I put in the batteries. The official Israeli channel has no reports of casualties. They're just talking about the new situation, what they call a general state of emergency, and the moderators, assisted by security officers, government officials and experts from academe, are trying to analyze the implications. There's nothing on the radio about an attack either, nothing on Iraq or on Syria. There's no mention of terrorists, except the story from this morning about an attempt that was foiled by our soldiers. Everyone agrees it's important not to take any chances, but nobody says a thing about roadblocks.

Outside, they've decided to roast all the defrosted meat. My mother says that's in bad taste. "This is no time for a barbecue. People might think we're celebrating when two families in the village have just come from burying their loved ones. Think of the contractor's mother. She kept fainting. Her son was the backbone of the family." Mother says she'll use a pressure cooker to prepare the meat. "It'll be much tastier, soft as a doughnut."

Father insists that the contractor was a complete idiot, only a fool would run a roadblock that way. "What was he thinking, that it's a game? What's a soldier supposed to think when a pickup comes charging straight at him? Isn't he bound to shoot?"

A car stops in front of the house and everyone stares at it. A young man gets out, one of the mayor's nephews. *"Salam aleikum,"* he greets us, and informs Father that the mayor has invited him to a meeting with the heads of all the families in the village, in the council building.

It's the first time they're having such a meeting. Normally, decisions are taken by council members without consulting the villagers themselves. Before the mayor's emissary has a chance to get back into his car, my father wants to know, "Has he decided to set up a security cabinet?"

Our family may be one of the smallest in the village, barely a hundred people, but my father has always been among the mayor's supporters. The two of them belonged to the Labor Party. The mayor followed in the footsteps of his father. His family is the largest in the village and the other heads of families had never succeeded in uniting and gaining power. When it comes to the local elections, the Muslims and the Communists and the nationalists don't stand a chance. The only thing that counts is the family. They all turn to their families, and what's good for the family is good for them.

The mayor has always been good at providing positions for the right people in the competing families, and ever since the state was established, there have only been two mayors, the father and the son. And like the father, the son began his party career by driving sanitation workers to the Labor Party head-quarters. Somehow they joined up with the right people, who realized that whoever was in charge of transportation belonged to one of the largest families, and that with a small amount of money they would succeed in bringing in thousands of votes. When the father was elected, he bequeathed his pickup and the sanitation workers to his eldest son, and when he died, he bequeathed his position as mayor.

Father and son looked very much the same. The father I know mainly from stories and from a black-and-white photograph I used to see all through high school. The high school was named after the late mayor, the current mayor's father. There was a large sign with his name and picture that greeted everyone who arrived at the school, and the same picture was positioned over the blackboard in every classroom, facing the students. I remember very clearly the day when the principal's father died, and the principal, who came from the second largest family in the village, one that supported a different Zionist party, removed the sign with the name of the late mayor and replaced it with one announcing that from that day on the school would be named after his father. A few minutes later a few of the mayor's relatives arrived. First they shot at the new sign, and then they took it down and replaced it with an even bigger sign bearing the name and picture of the former mayor, *Allah yirhamo*. Were it not for the intervention of some members of the Knesset and notables from the nearby villages, a feud would have broken out between the two largest families in the village. The compromise solution included naming the sports field for the principal's father. The principal refused at first, mainly because the village sports field is a patch of sand and the goalposts are nothing more than stones that the students keep replacing. The next day, the mayor installed proper goalposts, with nets. I remember how happy that made everyone, me too.

My father comes inside to get dressed for the meeting. He is always very careful with his appearance. I offer to drive him to the council building. Some of the grocery stores have closed already, having been cleaned out completely. My father looks through the window at the groups of people milling about in the streets, then looks at me and asks:

"Does it look serious to you, this whole thing?"

"I think it's scary."

"Yes, but it's just the second day. Why jump to conclusions? I bet the mayor's going to tell us he's been informed it's all over."

"I very much hope so."

"What do you think is going on?"

"I have no idea, Father."

I park outside the council building. Hundreds of people have gathered near the entrance, waiting for some news. Cars blasting music at full volume are cruising back and forth. I turn off the engine and stay in the car, light a cigarette, inhale and turn my head to blow the smoke out the window. A big new BMW pulls up and suddenly stops beside mine. There are four men inside. I don't recognize them, but I'm sure they're looking me over. The driver turns down the music, leans over the steering wheel and calls out my name. "*Wallah*, it's you. How've you been? It's been ages," he says, and smiles. Now I recognize him. He's Bassel, who was in my class.

I force a smile. I feel out of breath but stifle a cough. "You've started smoking, eh?" Bassel says, with a smile that hasn't changed at all. "It's bad for your health, you know," he goes on. *"Salamat."* Slowly he starts the engine and turns the music back up.

Over my desk in the children's room, they still have the framed picture from our class trip. I remember how I did everything I could to get Bassel to agree to have his picture taken with me. My God, what an idiot I was. By seventh grade, all the kids knew everything. They'd huddle together in groups during recess, whispering to one another, blushing. I was never accepted. I never managed to become one of the gang. Bassel was the leader. He talked more than anyone, and he was always the one who managed to get the other boys to listen. He had them in his grip. He could fascinate them and he could make them laugh. We'd have long lessons together in carpentry shop, and the teacher almost always gave us something to do, planing or woodcutting, and then he'd leave us alone. In the carpentry shop there were only boys. The girls took home economics in a kitchen. They cooked and baked cakes all year round. In the carpentry shop the boys allowed themselves to talk freely. Sometimes I'd hear words like erection, hair, mustache, pain in the chest. They'd raise their arms and compare armpits, some of them already had black hair growing there. Sometimes they'd pull down their pants and break out in laughter or shouts, which they quickly muffled before any of the teachers heard them. They'd pinch one another's chest and cringe.

In seventh grade there were three boys who were already shaving their mustache. Bassel was the first, and the other two imitated him. Everyone waited eagerly for the day they'd find black hair growing beneath their nose, and I was horrified at the thought that I would have to shave someday too. I don't want to do it, I told myself, I wish I never had any hair at all.

When I'd get home and find myself alone in my room or in the bathroom, I'd pinch myself in the nipples and convince myself that I couldn't feel a thing. Hair started growing in all sorts of places on my body, but it was still sparse. It scared me to death. What the hell does it mean? What are they talking about in class? And what is it about this change that they enjoy so much? Why do I find the new ache in my throat so disturbing? And what about the strange, broken voice I hear whenever I talk? It's as though I'm not me, as though it's the voice of some other guy I don't want to be, not yet. I don't want to be like everyone else, I'm not like everyone else, and things like that must never happen to me. Things like that happen to boys who get into trouble.

It wasn't only the boys that I hated because of the changes they were going through, but the girls too. There were already a few in our class whose breasts had swelled up, and when they raised their arms to answer a question you could see they were wearing bras, like my mother's. How could it be damn it? I hated every girl who wore a bra. I could spot them easily, I hated them, I was scared of them and I hoped they'd die.

Toward the end of seventh grade, almost all of the boys shaved their mustache, and even though I had black hairs that were longer than those of the other boys who were shaving already, I decided to keep pretending it wasn't happening. When the time came for final exams, I spent all my time studying and tried not to be distracted by anything. Except that one day, just before dawn, I woke up in a panic and knew I was peeing in my sleep. I couldn't help myself, no matter how hard I tried, and I felt my whole pajamas getting wet. What was happening to me? Very slowly I got out of bed without waking my two brothers, who were sleeping next to me. I went into the bathroom and discovered a large stain and didn't know what to do about it. I cried in silence, wiping myself off with toilet paper. The paper stuck to my skin and only made things worse. I went back into the room and pulled out a new pair of shorts and some clean pajamas. My wet clothes I put straight into the washing machine, not on the top but underneath, as far down as possible, under all the clothes. If my mother finds out, she'll kill me, I thought. The stickiness stayed with me even when I got back into bed.

When I discovered that the mattress was wet, I started sobbing in silence, lost and confused. I couldn't fall back asleep. I couldn't stop thinking feverishly about ways of concealing the terrible thing that had happened to me. I stayed in bed with my eyes open until morning, waiting for my brothers to leave the room, and only then got up. I could see the stain, and there was nothing I could do to erase it. I turned the mattress over, but that didn't solve the problem of the sheet. I had to get it into the washing machine too somehow. But what would my mother think if she discovered me taking a sheet to the wash for the first time in my life, and how was I going to explain what I was doing? I stuck my finger up my nose and scratched the inside till it started bleeding. I had hurt myself more than I'd intended to, and let the blood drip onto the sheet. I walked out of my room with the sheet carefully folded. You could see the blood, but not the stain. The blood covered my face. With one hand I held the sheet and with the other I tried to stanch the blood. My mother had a fright, and I explained that it happened sometimes. I hurried into the bathroom, shoved the sheet into the washing machine and rinsed my nose. Mother brought me some cotton and told me to hold my head back. She said it must be because of the heat, and she gave me a packet of cotton in case the bleeding started again while I was in school.

I was shaking all the way to school, holding my legs together more than usual so they rubbed against one another as I walked. I felt that the other kids making their way to school like me were laughing at me, figuring out the truth. I tried to get rid of those thoughts and to understand what the hell it was. I knew for sure that the answer had nothing to do with regular pee.

The following nights were especially tough. I tried not to fall asleep but it was no use. What I did do was remove the sheet before going to sleep and hide it under the blanket. If it happened again, at least I'd have a dry sheet so I could hide the stain on the mattress.

I did fine on the exams and got the highest grades in my class again. When they were giving out the report cards, the teacher made the whole class applaud me, which I didn't like at all.

He had dreamed up a new program where the stronger students would help the weaker ones over the summer vacation. How I hated the idea and how I hated the teacher at that moment. And even more than that, how I hated being teamed up with Bassel. That was all I needed, teaching English, Hebrew and math to the one student I hated the most in the whole class. The teacher knew we were neighbors with nothing but a fence between my home and his but I'd never visited Bassel and he'd never visited me. Even on days when we happened to leave for school at the same time, I'd stay some distance away from him, on the other side of the street, stepping up my pace to avoid him and the gang that followed him to school. Bassel didn't seem too happy at the idea either. He hated studying, and he certainly hated me too. But I'd always done whatever my teachers told me to do. I'd never dream of opposing anything they suggested.

We met twice a week at first, exactly as the teacher had ordered. He'd also made sure that Bassel's parents knew about the plan. They treated me with great respect, and his mother kept saying things like, "These are the young men you should be spending your time with. Why aren't all your friends like him, good students and respectful?" She always brought in a tray of cookies and something to drink, and made sure to keep Bassel's brothers and sisters out of the room so nobody disturbed him while he was doing his homework. Bassel didn't cooperate at all. I sat next to him and read to him from our schoolbooks and solved the math exercises, but he didn't seem the least bit interested. He was just waiting for the hour to be over so he could be rid of me.

He sat there, shaking his head in disgust at whatever I said, and never asked any questions even though I knew he hadn't understood a word of my explanations.

We'd sit there at the desk on our wooden chairs, not talking about anything except the homework. After a few sessions, things began to change. Bassel started asking me why I didn't shave like everyone else. Once he showed me how he shaved his mustache with his father's razor, and said it wasn't scary at all if you just know how to do it, and that you don't get cut, and that he could show me how if I wanted. He was even prepared to do it for me the first time. I said I'd rather not and that maybe I'd start in the summer vacation, before we went back to school. Gradually we began talking less and less about the homework, and our sessions became much more enjoyable. At first I pretended not to listen when he talked about girls and about the breasts that some of our classmates were developing.

I refused to go along when he asked me if I had any hair growing and if anything hurt in my chest or my throat. He would chuckle and say I was still a little boy, and slowly I began playing along with him, and enjoyed it. He pinched my chest, and it hurt so badly that I had to grimace. He laughed out loud when I said it didn't hurt. "Why are you so scared?" he asked. "It's that way with everyone." His parents did everything to make sure he got through school, but he always flunked at least three subjects. On one of the shelves in his room was a reference book titled *The Human Body.* Bassel said he'd show me all kinds of neat things, and he pointed to drawings of boys' and girls' bodies with their genitals showing. He began talking about erections and pointed to the drawings. He talked about the pleasure of it and the fun, and about how it completely distracts you from your schoolwork. He told me about his dreams, all about girls, and about how he'd wake up with the most wonderful feeling he'd ever felt, and his dick was hard and there was something coming out of it and that it's the best thing that ever happened to him.

I liked Bassel a lot. It was the first time I'd ever felt like I had a friend, the first time I understood that what was happening to me at night happened to other people too. He taught me to shove toilet paper into my underwear to prevent the staining and laughed when he heard I had thought I'd been peeing in my sleep. I couldn't believe I was telling him those things, couldn't believe I was telling anyone. I began enjoying those wet dreams too.

Bassel and I never discussed math again, or Hebrew language or English. All we talked about was our bodies. We pored over the book and I felt I knew everything. My way of thinking changed completely, and I let him shave off my mustache, after I'd asked my mother if it was all right. Instead of twice a week, we'd meet three or four times. Instead of one hour, we'd stay alone in that room for several hours. I told his parents he was progressing nicely and that he was even enjoying the lessons. They were delighted, and he told me that his father wasn't beating him as much since I'd arrived on the scene.

I felt really attached to him. I loved it when he laughed because of me, as if I were a little kid. He'd lock the door from the inside, take off his pants and his underpants and touch himself, with me watching. "See?" he'd say. "It's the greatest thing in the world." Then, at his request, I'd take off my clothes too, and he'd ask me to do the same thing. Sometimes he touched me himself. That's what everyone does, and me, what an idiot I was not to know anything about what the other boys in the class were doing. I did everything he asked; even when he told me to undress and he would rub against me from behind, I did it. I was glad to be giving him pleasure, glad I'd met him and that I could finally say I had a friend, and what a friend: Bassel, the boy that all the kids in class were afraid of, that they all tried to be nice to. Instead of his doing the homework I gave him, I'd do the homework he gave me. He promised, in return, that he'd share a desk with me the following year. At our last session, the day before school started, he asked me to get to school as early as possible and take the front desk for both of us. "Take the one right in front of the teacher," he said, "your favorite place."

I was so happy. I got to school before everyone and sat at the desk in front of the teacher. I put my bag down on the other chair, though that was unnecessary, since nobody really wanted to sit next to me. He'd arrive any minute now, and they'd see who I was sharing with. Bassel was one of the last to arrive, after the teacher had already come in. He was surrounded by his old cronies. I saw him in the doorway and gave him an enormous smile. I waved at him, and he laughed back. His whole gang laughed. He walked right past me, and I whispered, "Bassel, I reserved a place for you." He looked down at me and didn't say a word. Then he headed for his regular place at the back. I looked at him. He was just whispering something to the kids who were with him, and they looked at me and tried to stifle a laugh, to avoid being punished. He was moving his lips, and all I could make out was, "Asshole."

I sit there in the car. Bassel comes full circle in his BMW and drives back toward me. I see him in the mirror. I'm not going to look in his direction. He slows down as he passes me and honks. Unthinkingly, I turn to look. Four men are gazing at me and laughing. Bassel waves.

8

Dinner is ready. There's an enormous pot of cooked meat on the white plastic tablecloth outside, along with a big bowl of vegetable salad and a few other salads and spreads taken out of the fridge to be eaten before they spoil. We're waiting for Father to get back from town hall. A car pulls up at the front of the house and he gets out. His face is grim as he walks toward us. He greets us and takes his place at the head of the table without another word. Mother takes his plate and heaps meat onto it. "You haven't had anything to eat today, and the meat came out delicious."

We start eating and wait to hear Father's report on what transpired at the meeting. He doesn't volunteer anything, and finally I have to ask him.

"They decided to hand over the Gazawiyya and the *Daffawiyya*," the people from Gaza and the West Bank, Father says.

"They did?" my older brother asks. "Is that what the government got the mayor to do?"

"No," Father says. "The mayor has no idea what they want, but he figures, like everyone else, that the main concern of the police is the Palestinian workers. He's right."

"So what are they doing? Just how are they going to hand them over?" I ask.

"If the electricity stays disconnected till tomorrow morning and the roadblock stays in place, they'll hand over the illegal workers to the security forces. But only the adults, the ones over fourteen."

There are hundreds of workers from Gaza and the West Bank in the village. Many of them work for contractors from the village and others work inside the village itself, in construction, sanitation or gardening. They generally sleep on straw mats at the building sites, and a few lucky ones get to spend the night in large groups in warehouses belonging to their employers. In the past they could work inside Israel, but ever since the first Intifada they can no longer work there unless their employer has Israeli citizenship. In fact, workers coming from the cities and villages have become one of the most important sources of income for people in our village. Anyone who ever did a day's work as a construction worker has turned into a contractor, farming out work to people from Gaza or the West Bank, thanks to his Israeli citizenship. Besides the dozens of new "contractors" sprouting up in every Arab town and village inside Israel, many also transport workers to Tel Aviv, Netanya and other Israeli cities. Many of the drivers become their would-be sponsors. The workers clean, cook, work the assembly line, and the Israeli driver, the only person legally entitled to collect their salaries, distributes it after taking his fat cut. To a large extent, it is the inhabitants of the West Bank and Gaza are responsible for the prosperity of the village.

In other words, they are also responsible for the commercial boom. Once, before it all began, the Jews preferred to do their shopping in the cities of the West Bank, where they figured things were cheaper, and in fact things really were cheaper there. But since the Intifada began, about fifteen years ago, the Jews began to feel threatened and moved over to the Arab towns and villages within Israel itself, which were a little safer. For all intents and purposes, our village replaced two cities, Qalqilya and Tul-Karm. So as the condition of people on the West Bank got worse and worse, things were looking up for Israeli Arabs. The houses being built were unlike any we'd seen before. Businesses flourished and luxury cars could be seen outside almost every home in the village.

Besides the workers you could find hundreds of former West Bank and Gaza inhabitants in the village, people who'd managed to get Israeli citizenship once the Palestinian Authority was set up in the territories. In the past they had collaborated or had worked with the security forces, and they were now given a place to live in Arab villages within Israel, for their own protection. The local residents objected at first to the idea of harboring these traitors, but they soon discovered the economic advantages of hosting the new inhabitants. The Israeli government rented homes for them and paid well, and their purchasing power was nothing to sneeze at. Those people weren't being handed over; they were legal, after all, just like us.

The second Intifada was quite a problem. It undermined the whole economy and led to a deep recession, which affected everyone. Besides, the Jews were much less comfortable about driving into our village because of all the stories about the Islamic Movement and all the news programs that harped on how the Arabs were helping the terrorist organizations. Border Patrol squads had begun late-night raids. They'd swoop down on the warehouses and construction sites and detain workers who were defined as illegal. Now the mayor and the inhabitants of the village were volunteering to do this job for the state.

My father told us that all the heads of families had attended the meeting at the town hall. Some, the ones who were always opposed to the mayor, were opposed again, just as they'd object to building a new school simply because they were in the opposition and because of the long-standing animosity between families. But once the mayor explained that there was no choice, that if things went on this way for one more day there would be no drinking water left, they backed down. It turned out that the water pumps had stopped functioning when the power was cut, and that there was unlikely to be any water in the pipes by tomorrow morning. The mayor told everyone that this was why the sewage system wasn't working, and that pretty soon all of the homes would become stopped up, and people would have to start taking a shit outdoors, the way they used to long ago. He said that although people still had enough to eat, there wasn't enough money in the banks, so that some families wouldn't even have enough for bread. And those who did were too late, because there was no food left in the stores.

"And what did you say, Father?" I wanted to know.

"I said that we should go to prayers and that by tomorrow it would all blow over, but if there was no choice, there was no choice. Because we're not like them, we can't last long. This isn't Jenin, everything here is Israeli—the banks, the electricity, the water, the sewage, even the milk we drink comes from the Israeli dairies. We can't last more than two days here. If it goes on for a week, people will starve to death. They'll get dehydrated, they'll get sick."

"But who said the workers were the real reason for it all?"

"What else could they want? What other reason could there be? It's only the workers, they're the reason for it all."

My younger brother wants to know how the Communists reacted, and for a moment he's taken aback at his own question, but Father hardly notices and says that they objected at first, of course, because we're all one nation after all, but then they agreed too. And they weren't the only ones. "In the end, the decision was unanimous. Even the Islamic Movement agreed. Besides, what's the worst that could happen to them? If there were any who were wanted, they'd be detained, but they'd have been detained sooner or later anyway, in one of the raids. The ones who'd merely come to work would be taken back to their own villages. It's not as if we're pushing them into prison. Believe me, within two days they'll all be back here as if nothing happened."

We finish eating and there's a lot of meat left. Mother says it's a shame, and that if we want any more food today, we should come back.

9

I go home with my wife and daughter. My wife says it's not right to hand the workers over, that they have it so tough and that every time she sees them she feels sorry for them. The villagers have no compassion, do they, as if they don't have little children of their own and families to feed. What are they supposed to do now? Starve to death? My daughter goes back to sleep. My wife gets into bed and announces she's going to sleep for an hour or so, if she can possibly fall asleep at all in this heat with no air-conditioning. She says that if handing over the workers means we'll be able to turn the air conditioner back on, she's in favor, and she laughs. She doesn't take things seriously enough. Sometimes I envy her for the way she just accepts everything, just takes things for granted. In truth, nothing ever fazes her. She behaves as if everything is just going to be okay, and I realize there's no way I'll ever be able to share my anxieties with her. I'm sweating and I feel sticky. For a moment I consider getting in the bath, but I decide to wait. Mustn't waste water now. When I urinate, I don't even flush the toilet.

My wife falls asleep very quickly. I lie in bed beside her, my arms folded under my head and my eyes glued to the ceiling. I hear Farres, our neighbor. His voice has changed a little over the years, but I can still recognize him calling his children's names. Farres has an unusual accent, unlike that of most of the people in our village, and his family name is unusual too, but everyone refers to him as Farres the *Ramlawi* because his family came from Ramla. I'd heard not long ago that Farres had married a girl from Qalqilya and that he'd left Ibtissam. They hadn't actually gotten a divorce, but she didn't want to see him anymore.

I could hear Ibtissam, his wife, screaming at him to get the hell out of there. "What are you doing here, you piece of shit? Go back to your bitch." And Farres, with his accent, shouts that he wants to see his children. "I don't want to come in, just let me see them. I just want to see they're okay."

"Get the hell out of here. Nobody wants to see your face around here. Beat it before I call the police," Ibtissam yells.

Farres is calling his children by name now. "Muntassar, Haibbah." But they don't answer. Only Ibtissam keeps screaming and swearing at him.

When we were little, every now and then a whole family would descend on the village. All of their children would talk with strange accents, and suddenly, in the middle of the year, a new boy or girl would join our school, and we, the students, never liked them, those kids who talked funny. The teachers didn't like them very much either. In fourth grade we got this kid from Um el-Fahm. Everyone referred to him as *Fahmawi*. When we were in middle school, there was a girl from Lydda. We called her *Lydduya*. These kids always hung

146

out together and almost never exchanged a word with anyone else at school.

Everyone said it was the police that had brought them to the village. The *Fahmawi*, for instance, was said to be the son of a murderer, who'd killed someone in Um el-Fahm and was serving time. The police had moved the whole family because of the risk that someone would try to take revenge. When it came to the girl from Lydda they said her father was a drug dealer who had squealed to the police, so that people in Lydda were out to get him, and that was why the whole family had been moved to our village.

We knew we ought to be careful when it came to people with strange last names. Even our teachers always said that the police had forced the school to accept those kids. Otherwise they'd never have been admitted. Once the history teacher really screamed at the *Lydduya*, said they should just have stayed where they were, to die in Lydda, instead of being brought here to ruin our own children. The teacher said she was like a rotten tomato in a barrel, spoiling all the others. The whole class stared at the *Lydduya*, who was sitting on her own in the last row, standard procedure for the nonlocals. She burst into tears and clutched her head with both hands, but nobody took pity on her, even though she was a good student and was never out of line in class.

Farres the Ramlawi must be forty by now. He's been in the village for over fifteen years but he still speaks with a Ramlawi accent. I was in my second year in middle school when I heard his name for the first time. My parents were discussing the fact that our neighbor Ibtissam was going to marry the Ramlawi. I remember my mother was actually pleased, because maybe someone might get Ibtissam to pipe down. Ibtissam was quite old by then, over twenty-five, and everyone was sure nobody would ever marry her. Everyone said she was a little bit mad. She was forever fighting with the neighbors. My parents didn't really like her but they were always nice to her, to make sure she didn't throw any garbage at us or chop down the trees in our yard like she did to the other neighbors. She must have had about seven siblings, and they were all married by then. She had stayed on with her elderly father, who was wheelchair-bound and spent his time cursing the kids playing soccer across from their house. And however old he was, he was really strong and knew how to move fast in his wheelchair. We did whatever we could to keep our balls from falling in his yard, because he always sat outdoors, cursing and waiting for the balls, and when one did fall in his yard, he'd spring like a snake, wheelchair and all, lunging at the ball, clutching it in his arms, cursing and laughing gleefully, then go into the house to get a knife, and come up close to us to make sure we saw him rip the ball to shreds before handing it back.

Everyone hated him. He was the reason we weren't allowed to play ball outdoors at all, because somehow, sooner or later, the ball would land in their yard. Once, Khalil, our neighbor's son, tried to chase his ball after it fell into Ibtissam's father's yard. It was a new ball and Khalil said his father would kill him if he lost it. He ran as fast as he could, but no one could out-run the old man's wheelchair. Khalil didn't give up, despite the old man's screams, and jumped on him, crying, and struggled to prize the ball out of his arms. The old man wouldn't let go. He laughed in Khalil's face and promised to slash the ball with a knife. Khalil pulled at the ball with all his strength, and the old man fell out of his wheelchair and landed on the ground. Khalil, who had salvaged his ball, ran home. None of us dared approach the old man, who was crying uncontrollably, because we were afraid he'd beat us or stab us with his knife. He stayed there, on the ground, next to his overturned wheelchair, until Ibtissam got home and lifted him up. That day, she cursed everyone, and after her father told her it was Khalil who was to blame, she spent the next few hours swearing at him and his parents, then shattered their windows with big stones and promised to kill them unless they gave her father the ball. All of the neighbors tried to intervene and to get Ibtissam to let it go, but it was no use. In the end, Khalil's parents brought Ibtissam's father the ball. Khalil wept like a baby and promised that someday he would kill the bitch Ibtissam and her father, who ought to be dead anyway.

Everyone was pleased to hear that Ibtissam was getting married. The women had begun calling her the Old Worm who would never find a husband, and suddenly there was her man, coming from Ramla. They were sure that once she was married she would leave the neighbors alone. I remember that I went to her wedding too. I'd never seen Ibtissam happy before, but on that day she was dancing away in her white dress, with her father in his wheelchair, and kissing everyone. That was when I realized Ibtissam was actually a nice woman.

Farres the Ramlawi seemed like a good man, and the neighborhood rejoiced. They said he wasn't like the other strangers, he hadn't killed anyone, or if he had, it was his brother or his cousin who'd been involved in a murder in Ramla, and that Farres himself was a good person who'd once been a successful car mechanic before the police forced them to leave their home and move to our village.

My mother said that who knows, maybe someday there would be a *sulha* truce between the two families and then Farres and Ibtissam would move to Ramla for good, and that it would all be for the best. How much longer did the old man have anyway? My mother always said he was counting the days.

In fact, Ibtissam never left our neighborhood. One week after her wedding she came back home with Farres, and all the neighbors stood around looking at them as they entered their home with their luggage and a few pieces of furniture. Farres kept smiling and Ibtissam seemed very happy too. Later everyone said they must have made a deal: he would marry her and she would let him live in the house with her and her father. Her father died one month after she and her husband came back home, but she went on looking happy, as if his death hadn't really fazed her. She didn't get rid of the wheelchair. Just left it in the yard, and every now and then she'd sit in it and chase after our soccer balls.

It wasn't long before everyone hated the Ramlawi, and said that the old man had been an angel by comparison. My mother wouldn't let us talk to him, even if he called us. Initially he would invite all of the neighbors' children over to their house and he'd give us the ball and shout at Ibtissam if she tried to hold on to it. He seemed like a nice guy who liked children. Children would come to the house all the time. Some of them were older and some were in middle school, kids I knew. They would go into the house in groups of three or four, and Farres would always lock the door behind them.

My brothers and I never talked with Farres or Ibtissam. My father said he was a pervert, but we didn't know what that meant. Farres would stay home all day and never went to work. The groups of boys who came to see him kept growing larger. Sometimes they would knock on the door and Farres would open up and ask them to wait awhile, and they'd hang out in the yard until the previous group had left and Farres would invite the new group to come inside. He was always very nice, hugging them all and smiling at them: *"Ahalan u-sahalan."*

Once when we were playing soccer, Khalil told us that some of the kids in his class were going to Farres's place very frequently, that Farres would show them sex videos and let them smoke cigarettes and drink beer. Khalil said it cost five shekels to watch a film and another five for the beer and two cigarettes.

One day, Khalil's father, who was a teacher in the middle school, got really pissed off and started yelling at his students as they approached Farres's home, warning them not to go inside. "I'll tell your parents," he yelled. "I know you. Just wait and see what I do when you get to school tomorrow." The kids got out of there as fast as they could, and Farres kept coming out onto the balcony, smiling and taunting Khalil's father. "You're interfering with my work." And Khalil's father yelled back, "Is this what you call work? You should be ashamed of yourself." And Farres said it was a shame that Khalil's father didn't show more respect to a cinema professional like himself.

PART FOUR

Sewage

1

In the evening, several hundred young men are recruited to get the job done as quickly as possible. All those who'd spent the morning waving green flags and red flags and Palestinian flags have volunteered to round up the illegal workers. In vans, cars and trucks, they're doing whatever they can. The noise of the engines fills the dark village streets, with nothing showing except headlights. The operation began late at night, but still, many people are awake, peeping out of their windows, staring from their balconies, sitting in their yards and looking on. Some are even cracking sunflower seeds. The whole family has congregated in my parents' home again. The two children—mine and my brother's—are sleeping in my parents' bed. My younger brother is trying to study by candlelight, straining to prepare for the exam the following morning, but finally he gives up. From time to time we hear the wail of a siren or the sound of someone screaming, probably egging the workers on. Why the hell can't they at least go about it less callously?

The car radios in the vehicles driven by the village youth are playing loud music, and the drivers are honking rhythmically to signal they're transporting workers. They're rounding them all up in the yard of my wife's school, not far from our home. Every now and then my mother, who's feeling uncomfortable about the whole thing, curses the Jews. My wife says the villagers are behaving like animals. She says they are animals, and always have been. Why did they have to choose the most repulsive people for the job? Couldn't they have done it quietly, by persuasion? Couldn't they at least say they were sorry? Luckily, being Arabs, they're not drafted into the Border Police or the army. They'd make the most brutal soldiers in the world.

My heart is beating hard, and my head is about to burst. We stay at my parents' home until late at night. Finally the noise of the cars stops and it seems like the job has been completed. The only remaining noise is coming from the schoolyard nearby. Occasionally we hear one of the workers shout, *"Haram aleikum,"* but someone soon snaps at him to shut up. My father has never looked so defeated. You can see him in the candlelight, sitting in his white plastic chair with tears streaming down his face.

We leave our daughter with my parents. My wife falls asleep right away, right after her shower. I don't have the heart to shout at her, even though it really was irresponsible of her. How the hell could she sleep so well? I try to fall asleep too but it's no use. I pace the house for hours. From time to time I lie down on the bed, shut my eyes and then get up again, go up on the roof and look at the blue headlights of the jeeps. I light a cigarette and listen to the engines running, much louder than before. I wonder if the workers at the school have been able to sleep at all.

2

Three buses, belonging to the company that used to transport the workers to work and back belong to one of the richest men in the area, are lined up at the gate of the schoolyard at daybreak. I can see them from our rooftop, loading up the workers—more than one hundred in all. A few armed thugs get on each bus to keep an eye on them. I get the car and head toward the road that leads out of the village. To my surprise, thousands are waiting, dressed for work, they're convinced that once we hand over the workers they'll be free to leave. The mayor, the village council members and a few of the village dignitaries are standing at the exit, also waiting for the buses.

The workers get out, their heads down, and march in the direction the villagers point to. From time to time, one of them sobs and begs for pity. The mayor orders his men to line up the workers. More and more troops join the two tanks standing six hundred feet away, and the soldiers get into position and point their weapons. The mayor waves a white flag and shouts as loud as he can that they're handing over the illegal workers. A council member takes a bullhorn, the one they used the night before to shout anti-Israel slogans, and yells out their intentions. The soldiers don't respond. The mayor orders the workers to put their hands up and tells the first one to hold up the white flag in his right hand. Two young men place planks across the barbed wire so the workers can walk across. The first worker, tall and thin, climbs up onto the plank. He is shaking, and he starts staggering across. As he approaches the other side, he takes a bullet, lets out a half shout and drops to the ground. He's been hit in the heart. The workers all duck, and some get down on the ground. The workers start yelling and crying, and try to escape to the rear, but they're blocked by the villagers. The mayor shouts into the bullhorn that nobody will be allowed to leave. The workers sob and plead for their lives. I stand to the side, at a distance, bent over, breathing hard and making sure to stay out of range. I see Mohammed, the harelip. He looks the least concerned of any of them. The mayor and his aides decide to try again, apparently convincing themselves that the soldiers had only shot because they thought one of the workers was hiding explosives under his clothing. The mayor gives his orders and the sobbing workers are stripped brutally by thugs and by others who've always hated them. The workers who try to resist are kicked hard in the ribs. They curse the whole time, are slapped and clubbed and are made to line up again, wearing nothing but underpants.

The mayor chooses one of them, who may look a little older than the rest, and orders him to go to the head of the line. The worker pleads, bends over, sobs, asks for pity in the name of God, and the mayor explains there's no choice. "It's all because of people like you," one of the local young men shouts at him. "You wanted al-Aqsa, didn't you? Well, you're on your own. Just look what a mess you've made for us."

Trembling all over, practically naked, the first worker climbs up onto the planks, carrying a flag in his hand. He tries to cross over, step by step, slowly, getting down on all fours and inching his way forward over the body of the first worker who was shot. Another shot is heard. The second worker doesn't move. He's lying on top of the first one. A great cry cuts through the air. The workers begin shouting with all their might, heart-rending cries, weeping and sobbing. Many of the villagers are shouting too. "*Haram*, enough, they don't want them." More and more people arrive at the scene. Women too. The older women, who are supposed to wear a white kerchief, rush toward the roadblock, crying and begging for the workers to be allowed to leave, protecting them with their own bodies. They shout at the mayor and his men and swear that God should make them burn in hell. They grab the planks that have been laid across the barbed wire and try to use them to pull away the two bodies. The body of the second worker, the one in underpants, falls over to the other side. The women succeed in pulling in the first one. The men all move away. Only the women and children remain. The workers, weeping, gather up their clothing. Nobody speaks to them.

The commotion at the entrance is over. Just a few children remain, patrolling near the roadblock on their bikes and watching the soldiers and the tanks. I walk back, passing by the fountain that the mayor had dedicated with much pomp and circumstance, which was supposed to welcome the Saturday shoppers into the village. The fountain isn't working. There's no electricity. The water seems dirtier than ever. Cans and cigarette butts and other trash thrown in by the thousands who have huddled at the village entrance over the past two days are floating on the water.

Shopkeepers are standing in the doorways of their stores watching the crowd and waiting to find out what's going to happen. The shops aren't exactly open for business. Almost all of them make do with a small opening, by lifting the metal barrier only partway. That way the shopkeepers will be able to lock up in a hurry if the mayhem starts again. They're here out of habit, but they came knowing perfectly well that they won't be selling any furniture or appliances today. One of them, tall and fat, about fifty years old, is standing in the doorway of his grocery store holding a cup of coffee. I walk toward him, and when he sees me he asks from a distance, "What are you looking for?"

"Cigarettes."

"Don't have any," he says, and rubs his hands together to indicate there's almost nothing left.

The green garbage pails bearing the signature of the local council are fuller than ever. Their lids have been removed and the residents can pile up pyramids of garbage. There are heaps of garbage all around. There's no more fuel for the garbage trucks. The farther you go up the street leading into the village, the higher the garbage, and the stench grows stronger with every step you take. Big bags of meat and dairy products that have gone bad have been thrown in the garbage or placed nearby. Swarms of flies, as well as cats and dogs, are fighting over the new treasures, more bountiful than anything they'd dared to expect in this village.

3

I soon discover how badly I miscalculated when I decided to take a shortcut home by cutting through the village center. There's no escaping the putrid smell coming from the piles of garbage that almost block off the little alleyways winding between the old homes in the village center, many of them a hundred years old or more. I try not to breathe through my nose and to take quick little breaths, holding the air in my lungs for as long as possible. What's happened to these people? The garbage isn't collected for one day and the village turns into one big dump? Never mind the ones who put out their garbage the day before, thinking it would be collected as usual. The real problem began with those big, ugly women with their heads covered in a kerchief, who just go on putting out their garbage and piling it higher and higher in the doorways. They must think of themselves as people with good hygiene. Why don't the neighbors take some initiative and clean the neighborhood? Why don't they move the garbage farther away to the outskirts of the village, for heaven's sake? What are they thinking?

The children haven't gone to school today and they're using the day off as an opportunity to roam barefoot among the garbage pails, playing tag and hide-and-seek. A group of men huddle in an alleyway and surround two village council workers in blue coveralls who have come to deal with the sewage overflowing. The smell grows worse as you get closer. Some of the men cover their noses and watch the city workers trying to fix the problem, but to no avail. I hear one of them say there's nothing to repair. The village sewage has been blocked from the outside, and they'll have to wait till the powers that be unblock the pipe. This explanation doesn't go over well with the crowd and some of them start shouting at the guys in the coveralls, saying they don't know how to do their job. One of them takes advantage of the opportunity to curse the village council for not clearing the garbage. "Instead of handing over the Palestinian workers," a large, middle-aged man in a *gallabiyeh* says, "you should have let them fix the garbage and the sewage. They're much better at it than you are." All the others laugh as if they've just heard a particularly amusing joke.

The café at the outskirts of the older part of the village is packed. Men of all ages fill the inner room and the courtyard. Many have nowhere to sit and they settle for drinking a cup of tea or coffee in plastic cups while standing up. At some of the tables, four men are playing cards. There's no work today either, and nothing much to do except wait for the closure to end. The local workers woke up early out of habit, if they got to sleep at all, to check what happened after the West Bank workers had been handed over to the soldiers—hoping to hear they could now resume life as usual. Once they understood that the mayor's plan had failed, there wasn't much left for them to do, and a game of cards coupled with some café chitchat seemed like the ideal way to get through another day of idleness.

A group of high school students who've gathered at the school decide to stage another march, except that this time nobody is eager to join them. No more than a few dozen people take part. From time to time, one of them tries to lead the others in a refrain of protest cries, but this soon dies out. When they realize that their rally is doomed to fail, the students disperse and head home. They don't even get as far as the roadblock at the entrance to the village. The old men go on sitting at the mosque, rolling tobacco. At the nearby cemetery the Palestinian workers are digging two graves. In one, they bury the worker that the women had managed to pull back. As for the one on the other side, all they can do is throw his clothing over the fence into the grave. They don't cry. The burial takes place in silence and prayer.

At the entrance to the cemetery I see the lupinus seeds vendor. I haven't seen him for years, with his green cart, the same one he used when I was still in elementary school. Nobody knew what his real name was. Everyone just called him Thurmus, the local word for lupinus. He used to show up every day when school got out, equipped with a tape recorder that he'd position next to his big bowl of thurmus seeds, and play his Egyptian songs. Everyone made fun of Thurmus. He looked strange, and his eyes would follow you everywhere. His eyes followed the shoppers even as he was scooping up the warm thurmus seeds from the vat and filling the bowls. He never missed the bowl, even though his gaze wasn't focused on what

164

he was doing. He'd stare right through you, never smiling, never talking with anyone. I was scared of him at first, and I wasn't the only one. But everyone bought thurmus from him because it really was the best.

I can see him now, standing at the entrance to the cemetery, his tape recorder playing the same songs, songs which used to be hits and nobody remembers anymore, waiting for the workers to finish the burial rites. Maybe he'll manage to sell them some thurmus. In earlier times, he'd walk the streets all day, seeking out the crowds, the big events, pushing his green cart. His favorite sales spot was the soccer field. He'd show up not only at the Saturday games of the adult team but at all the practice sessions too, including those for the junior team.

I remember he never missed a single practice, not even of the junior team, when I was playing on it. I wasn't exactly playing, I was signed up, and I came to every practice, always on time. I didn't like soccer, but I treated it as another subject I had to excel at. Like math, or carpentry, or religion. The kids on the team said the only reason the coach agreed to take me was that he was afraid my father would get him fired. I could never find a partner when we were supposed to divide into pairs. The coach always had to force one of the kids to pair up with me. I'm not sure I was such a bad player, actually, but I hated those practice sessions, hated coming to the soccer field and hated the kids on the team. I didn't want to upset my father by quitting. He always said, *"Mens sana in corpore sano."* And he'd repeat it over and over again. I remember him telling me once, "Maybe you don't run as fast as the others, maybe you don't kick as hard as they do, but you're smart and you should decide how the game is played." But that's bullshit. The best players were the ones who ran faster than everyone and kicked harder than everyone. They never invited me to play in the games that took place in the village. I was always on the bench, a backup, except I never got to replace anyone. But I had a team shirt, with the logo of a cement factory splashed across it. The factory belonged to the father of one of the kids on the team. The kids said they bet my father had had to buy me the shirt, but I didn't take it to heart. I knew they were just jealous.

I remember that Saturday morning when the group was supposed to play its very first away game. Everyone was talking about how we'd be taking a bus to play against the Jews in a real junior league game. The coach ordered us to show up at the field at nine A.M. I got there first. The second to arrive was Thurmus with his cart. I kept my distance from him, and just went on observing him. If he comes closer, I thought, I'm out of here as fast as I can go. The coach and the minibus arrived before the rest of the team. I was the first to get on, wearing the red uniform of the team and regulation shoes. Slowly the bus started filling up. The coach asked me to get off for a minute, said he needed to talk to me. "Bring your bag with you," he said. The coach explained that the minibus was too small and there wasn't room for everyone, and the cement-factory owner had decided to come along too. "Next time we'll take you along," he said, and got on the bus. I managed to control myself, didn't show a thing. I was about to explode but I didn't say a thing. I could see the kids laughing from inside the bus, looking at me, and I knew they were talking about me, but I showed nothing, I kept it bottled up. Only when the bus drove off did I feel I couldn't take it any more. My shoulders shook, and even though I tried hard not to cry, the tears just streamed down.

"This is for you," I heard a voice from behind me. Thurmus was standing there with a cup in his hand. "Take it, it's for you. Don't cry. I've seen you play. You're good. I've seen you."

I look at Thurmus now, the only person who came to the funeral. I wait to catch his gaze, to see the big eyes following me. But no, his head is lowered and his big body is trembling.

4

The piles of garbage in our neighborhood are smaller than elsewhere, mainly because the neighborhood is at the edge of the village and a little less crowded than the ones in the center. But it's still difficult to ignore the stench. Our sewage hasn't clogged up yet, but it will soon. Women in *dishdashes* keep sweeping and cleaning their houses. I step up my pace as I walk toward my parents' home. My wife and my brother's wife are back from school already. Very few children came to class today, and the principals, who met with the mayor early in the morning, decided to send everyone home. Nobody dared to use the term *strike* for the day off they'd been forced to take. Nobody wanted to have to answer to the Ministry of Education later on.

My father is sitting in the yard. He has the chess set in front of him and is just about to arrange the pieces for a game. His cousin Salim will be arriving soon, as he does every morning. Everyone at home knows by now that the handing over of the workers hasn't done the trick, and that the roadblock is still in place. My younger brother has gone back to sleep. My older brother is at the bank. My mother and her two sisters-in-law are in the kitchen peeling potatoes. I look at them, and see the pity in their eyes, because they know what happened and that I saw it all. I don't have the strength to speak. I only tell them there's no more water and that the sewage has begun overflowing in a few places, and that we shouldn't use anything connected to the drainage system. I know they're waiting for an explanation. This latest piece of news worries them. I go into the children's room and spread out on my boyhood bed. I look at my brother, who's only half asleep. Our eyes meet, but we don't say anything. I can hear the women in the kitchen, amused at my mother's announcement that from now on all peeing will be done in the yard.

The images rush by me in rapid succession—the workers in their underpants, the roadblock, the reverberating sounds, the shooting, the yelling at the rallies, the smell of garbage everywhere. Because of the heat, stifling by now for lack of air-conditioning, all the doors and windows in the house are open, letting in the filthy air.

I should be in my office right now. I've missed my final opportunity to get a story into the weekend supplement. I've got enough material for a big one. How I've missed writing full-length stories. The deadline for supplement stories is right now, Tuesday morning. They're about to lay it out and this evening they'll send it down to be printed. I wonder if the written media are as oblivious as the electronic ones to what has been going on. I suppose they are. If there's been a gag order issued, it applies to all the media. I'm glad, actually, to know there may have been a gag order because it means no one will have written anything on the subject, and maybe I'll get a chance to do a big spread next weekend.

I miss my chair, my workstation, my position. I miss the black coffee in the disposable cups, the secretary's smile when I pass her on my way to the kitchenette. I even miss the shouting of the editor reminding me about my deadline. I miss the people I share an office with. I wonder what they're thinking, if any of them have missed me, if they feel sorry for me. Everyone must know what's going on here. Everyone must have seen the gag orders by now, delivered by fax and treated as sacred.

I wonder if any of them are concerned about me. I can picture them sitting around sipping their coffee, talking about me, laughing as they always do, making fun. I can picture the fashion writer who's taken my spot, who uses my keyboard, my phone, my ashtray.

How I hate them now, how I hate myself for trying to believe I was really one of them, for trailing after them on lunch breaks, for trying to kid around with them, to make them laugh. I never managed to feel like I was one of them. They always made me feel like an outsider. I hate myself now for not doing a thing about it all this time, for letting things get this way. Didn't I realize we'd find ourselves in a situation like this sooner or later? Not that I really know what kind of a situation this is exactly.

I hate myself for thinking that coming back to the village would solve anything. For some reason, I thought that if I was surrounded by people like myself, my own people, nothing bad could happen to me. I thought that in the village I'd be much more sheltered than I was in the Jewish neighborhood. I thought the village would make a good guesthouse for me to come back to at the end of my working day, like everyone else. I'd go off to work and I'd come back to sleep, safe and sound. But now I have no choice but to admit that there's nowhere to run away to anymore. I hate myself for not getting out of here at the right time, for finding comfort in the thought that everything would work out soon. I hate myself for not getting my wife and daughter out of here as soon as I felt the danger approaching, as soon as the hatred began getting to me, day in and day out, at work, in the street, at home, in restaurants, in the malls and in the playgrounds.

I should have left everything behind and made my way to a sane country, anywhere. But like an idiot, I had preferred to go back home to my parents and to ignore the warning signals. I knew Arabs are hated everywhere. I knew that being an Arab is the worst thing that could happen to a person nowadays. The xenophobia they have in Europe couldn't possibly be as bad as what we have here. It just couldn't be.

There is no choice now, no escape. And I can't afford to waste time crying over things I should have done but didn't. I've got to pull myself together and do what has to be done. I've got my work cut out for me. I've got to survive.

My father's regular chess partner has arrived, and they can be heard outside, arguing at the top of their lungs. "You touched it, you moved," my father is saying. "That was an accident," his partner says. "What's got into you today?"

I sit up in bed, rubbing my eyes with my fists. I take a deep breath, and the stench makes me cough hard. My younger brother sits up too. "What's that smell?" he asks. "God help us!"

"They aren't collecting the garbage anymore. They don't have fuel for the garbage trucks. The truth is that the village dump is over the fence put up by the soldiers."

"This is serious business, isn't it? What do they want?"

"I don't know."

"I heard they shot two workers. God, look how far we've gone. I'm ashamed to be part of this village. Of this community, of this people. Know what? We have it coming. It was obvious a long time ago that we needed to put up a fight, to throw stones at them at least. Look what we get for our exemplary behavior. It's a disgrace."

"Listen, this isn't the time to start analyzing where we went wrong. We were wrong, and that's that. Let's not waste any more time. Pretty soon we're going to run out of water. I need you to help me, okay?"

"Are you serious? Do you think it's going to last much longer?"

"I don't know. I wish I did, but we can't take any chances. They're not pumping in any more water. All we have is what's left in the water tanks on the roof. That's it. We can't waste it. From now on, water is for drinking only. Besides, I'd like you to come with me for a drive around the village."

My brother doesn't ask too many questions. He gets off the bed, a head taller than me, much thinner and more athletic. He puts on an undershirt, puts his hair in a ponytail, ties it with a rubber band, slips on his sandals and signals to me that he's ready to go.

My mother is in the kitchen making tea. I restrain myself from yelling. I must not lose my cool now and get everyone worked up. They already think I'm overreacting, as usual. "Mother," I call out to her, and my wife and sister-in-law listen from their seats at the kitchen table. "Mother, you know the water supply is running low and God only knows how much longer it will last. So please, go easy on the tea, and for heaven's sake don't start cleaning the house like our idiot neighbors. Better keep the water for drinking."

Mother stares at me as if I've gone mad. As if the idea that we could run out of water too has never occurred to her. We've had several special alerts in emergency situations—before the October War, on Land Day, during the first Gulf War, at the beginning of the Intifada. Then too people bought out the food stores, to be on the safe side. Except that nobody ever thought in terms of running out of water. Especially since there was never any interruption in the water supply, which came from Israel. There were never any real shortages. This war is different from all the others.

My brother disappears for a few minutes, then returns. "I went up on the roof," he says. "The water tank is half empty already. What's used up is used up, and no more water is coming in." Everyone is taken aback at my brother's announcement. Now I can count on their taking things a bit more seriously. To make sure they don't become overly upset, I remind them that there are water tanks on my roof too and on my older brother's—tanks which are even bigger than the ones on my parents' roof. "If we use the water sparingly, it can last for two weeks. But we have to be careful. Which means you can't even flush the toilets. So, Mother, you've got to go easy on the coffee and tea, even if Father gets uptight. Let Salim go have tea in his own house if he wants to."

I leave, and my brother follows. My fuel tank is almost full. I get in the car and turn on the radio. My brother sits next to me and laughs at me for buckling up. "As if you're going to get a ticket from the cops patrolling this village," he says. They're playing happy music on the army radio station. "At least in the car you can turn on the air conditioner," my brother says, and I tell him he can open the window because I don't intend to waste fuel.

There's nothing unusual in our neighborhood. Even the grocery store is open, and I remember that I owe them some money. I stop the car, turn off the engine and go in. "Anything new?" the owner asks me. I shake my head and pull out my near-empty wallet. "How much do I owe?" The owner goes inside and I follow him. It's dark in there, and it takes him a while to find my card. I walk through the aisles. There's no food left. No candles or batteries either. Just cleaning supplies, toilet paper and the disposable dishes they sell before a holiday. I walk past the refrigerators. The shelves are completely empty. Everything would have spoiled anyway, but it stands to reason that people were so worried that they bought it all. I bend over to the bottom of one refrigerator, grab the thick handles and open the bottom compartment, with its extra-thick doors.

I'm thrilled. I knew it. People just didn't think about the fact that they'd be needing water and sodas too, and there are a few bottles left. I take as many as I can carry and ask the shop owner to add them to my bill. Bottles of Coke, orange juice and the mineral water that hardly anybody buys unless it's for infants, on doctors' orders. My brother sees me approaching the car and gives a big smile. I signal him to go inside and get some more, and stuff everything into the trunk. My brother goes inside and returns with a few more bottles. Suddenly the shop owner yells, "Hey, what do you think you're doing?"

"What? We're buying some drinks. We're having a party," my brother tells him.

"No, please do me a favor. Don't take everything. Leave a few for me."

"You've got more in the refrigerator," my brother says, and keeps walking toward the trunk.

I pay the owner for the purchase and thank him. He looks to see how much is left in the fridge. "What? You've only left me three bottles?"

"If you need any Coke, just come over," my brother says. "Besides, you're invited to the party. I'm getting engaged."

"Congratulations," the owner says. He's feeling a little less uptight now.

We make the rounds of the stores. Most are closed, and there's nothing useful in most of the ones that are still open. Every now and then we find a soft drink bottle on the lower shelf of a refrigerator. We manage to get hold of about twenty bottles. And every time my brother comes back with a bottle, his smile grows larger, as if we've managed to pull one over on the whole world. I begin enjoying the game too, for some reason. My brother's smiles flatter me. He chuckles at the thought that things will go back to normal in half an hour and we'll get stuck with enough drinks to last us a whole year. "In the end, I really will have to get engaged to get rid of all this Coke and juice," he says.

We walk the village streets, which are filling up with people who have nothing to do. Bitter-looking people stare at the piles of garbage, look at each other and don't know what to do. We can see the sewage streaming through the streets, the flow getting wider and wider. There are blockages all over the village and I wonder how it's possible for people to know that the sewage is stopped up and the village has no water—and to continue behaving normally. Sometimes I can't help feeling unspeakably sorry for them when I see how much they believe in their citizenship.

"Where now?" my brother asks.

"Let's load up two gallons of cooking gas."

"What, do you think we're going to run out of that too?"

"I don't like taking chances."

5

My father walks around outside of the house with a spade in his hand, drawing circles in the blazing sand. It's amazing how he can still find the exact location of the sewage pipes. I could never have done that, even though I was old enough when they connected us to the system and was standing next to my father when they dug the ditches and laid the pipes and covered them up. The water level in the toilets and in the sinks in my parents' house is rising. Nobody is checking the situation yet but one can deduce that the same thing will happen soon enough in my brother's house too, and in mine. My younger brother and I join my father, who digs down slowly until he reaches concrete. The filthy water has risen above the first covering. My father asks us to find a crowbar with which to lift the cover. He makes a circle where the next cover should be and gently pushes away the sand with his spade. "Same mess here," he says. "I bet all of them are blocked up. The problem is in the central system, not here." My brother gets a crowbar and tries to find an opening along the edge of the lid so he can pry it open. He doesn't do too well, and tries a different spot. Eventually he succeeds in forcing it in, but the lid is too heavy, too stuck, and he can't pry it loose. I take over and try to help him, using as much force as I can. The lid shifts a little but slips back into place. Father shouts at us from a distance and urges us to keep trying. "Come on, what is it with you, two men fighting with one drain cover?"

The two of us try to do it together. My brother laughs out loud. We take turns kicking it, shoving the crowbar along its edge. Finally it gives. The ditch is completely flooded, and water is spilling out. The smell isn't that bad, and it doesn't get any worse.

My father says there is no point draining a single ditch. "Everything is stopped up. The whole village must be stopped up by now. The problem isn't here. There isn't much we can do." My father is very handy in situations like this. The truth is we've never had to call in a plumber or a painter or an electrician. I have no idea where he acquired these skills. You could easily assume he'd once worked in the sanitation department or with an electrician. For as long as I can remember, whenever that kind of problem came up, Father would roll up his sleeves and set about solving it and we, the three brothers, would follow him, as would-be apprentices trying to live up to their master's high standards.

He stands there for a moment, leaning on his spade, looking this way and that, his eyes shining at the thought of the new challenge that has come his way. He looks up at the houses he's built for us and says, "Lucky I used a provisional connection to hook you up to the sewage system. We saved money and I also knew it would save you unnecessary work. He smiles as he recalls how he managed to connect the whole system in a single night, laying out the pipes and connecting them to the parents' house. He said at the time that there was no point paying the municipality more money and that, besides, that's what everyone does. He did pay once, after all, and that should be enough.

So there is no blockage. The sewage is backing up, in fact, because the entire village is blocked. My father looks up from his spade, his face pensive as if trying to solve a complicated riddle, and he says, "There's nothing we can do about it. We've got to block off the last drainage ditch, the one from the house to the central system. Let's start out by doing that." He shouts to my mother to come outside. She hurries out, wearing the kerchief usually reserved for days of mourning. Father instructs her to bring some plastic bags and the sack of gypsum from the storeroom. My mother hurries into the house and comes back with the supplies Father has asked for. Meanwhile, he brushes the sand off the last covering, the one closest to the road. One movement of Father's hand is enough for my brother and me to understand he wants us to lift the lid. We both get into position. This time I am the one who looks for a place to insert the crowbar. Father watches disparagingly. I find the spot, shove it in with all my strength and give it a powerful kick, sending the crowbar up in the air. Father covers his head. I scurry backward.

"Are you a complete idiot?" he shouts. "Are you trying to kill us?" My younger brother laughs, picks up the crowbar and tries his luck. It works. He presses down, using his full body weight to dislodge the lid. It moves and I hurry to catch it from below before it slips back into place. "Yuck!" I say as I lift it up, my hands suddenly coated with green slime. I shake my head and rush home to wash my hands. But then I remember the water shortage and I'd better put it off till we're through. "It's just as well that you got yourself dirty," my father says. "It's about time." The last ditch lets loose a stronger outpouring of sewage, with repulsive turds floating on top. I can't hold back. I bend over and puke. My bones hurt, my face is flushed and I throw up again and again. I hold my hands as far away from my body as I can. My eyes are burning and filled with tears and my nose is running. There isn't much I can do except wipe my face with the shoulder of my shirt.

"As long as you've gotten dirty," my father says, and hands me a plastic bag filled with a white mixture, "shove your hand into the ditch and push this bag into the pipe that goes toward the street so we don't wind up with the sewage of the entire village. Got that? Not the pipe going toward the house, the one going in the direction of the village."

I retch one more time, making gagging sounds. It hurts as much as before but nothing comes out anymore. I can tell by my brother's expression that he's feeling very sorry for me, and he signals to let me know that he'll do it instead. I shake my head and approach the ditch, where I see the sewage flowing in all directions. I bend over without thinking twice, my knees digging into the ground, which by now has turned into a smelly bog. With one hand I lean on the ground, and the other hand I push in, deep into the ditch. My entire arm is inside by now, as I grope for the pipe that Father was talking about. I find it easily, and keep pushing. My whole left arm is inside the pipe. My cheeks are up against the muck. I don't think about it at all, don't think about anything, just keep looking at my father, who stands there smiling and tries to speed things up, looking every bit the winner.

I proceed like a robot, tilting my face to the right to keep my mouth and eyes from touching the sewage. I shove the bag into the pipe and inform my father. I pull out my arm. It's dripping wet, but I ignore that. My father hands me a bag slightly larger than the first one and says we need to insert one more to make sure it's completely blocked. "It mustn't flow back up from the ditch near the road." I take it from him without a word and stoop back down, resuming the same position, my left arm reaching all the way in, my left cheek and whole body touching the ground. And I push the bag, which is harder to do because this one is larger.

"Now we've got to get the sewage out," my father says, and hands me and my younger brother some black buckets. "Pour it out in the road, or as close as possible to the road." The sun is centered high above us, but we can't stop now. We have to finish the job. Empty one ditch, the one that the sewage of the three neighboring houses will flow into. My brother and I take turns plunging the bucket into the ditch, and pulling it out when it's full, moving a few steps back and pouring it as close as possible to the road near the house. A few of the neighbors see us and try to do the same, to deal with their own sewage problems. "Let's see how long it takes them to figure out that they have to block off the pipe to the road first," my father says, smiling his victory smile. My brother and I work continuously, without speaking, quickly, ignoring the heat and the stench. The level of the water in the ditch remains unchanged. My father walks over to the ditches we uncovered earlier. He studies the first, then the second, and announces loudly, "Excellent, it's beginning to go down. Soon it will be over."

I try to think about the new situation, the roadblock, and wonder if I should be listening to the news. Maybe they've found out something, maybe things have changed, but I can't really concentrate on such things. My main concern now is to dump my bucket, which is full of muck. My father gets back in position. He calls out my mother's name, and then, "Water!" at which she emerges with a glass of water in her hand. He complains it isn't cold, spills it out, hands the glass back to her and asks for another. She reminds him that they no longer have a refrigerator and that she can't make it any colder—which earns her a tirade from Father, who doesn't care about anything right now, and she should have thought of it sooner. Everyone has to obey Father. Mother is his main victim, but at least she enjoys it. She adores him, loves him more than her own life. She'll do anything to keep him from getting upset, and it isn't that she's afraid of him. Unlike us—we have always obeyed him to keep from being punished. I dash back and forth with the bucket, glancing at Father every now and then, to see if he is at least pleased with my hard work. But his face shows nothing.

What am I afraid of, for heaven's sake? I'll be thirty soon. What am I afraid of? A punishment? It's been ten years since he last struck me. My mother returns with another glass of water, and warns him apologetically that there is no ice, no refrigerator and it's as cold as she can make it. Impatiently, he grabs the glass from her and drinks it, grumbling, muttering garbled words. My body is overcome with fear, not because of the situation in the village, and not because of the roadblock or the lack of food and water, but because of my father's anger. I've always tried to do as he asked, but I haven't always succeeded, and whenever I failed to do something, like pulling out the weeds under the trees which once grew where the new houses now stand, or when my grades weren't good enough, I'd get a beating. I can still hear the sound of those lashings, of the branches he'd use to flog me.

The floggings with tree branches were not the most painful punishment I received, but they were the harshest ceremony of all. Father would decide on the punishment. He didn't just lash out in a fit of fury or irritability. He planned the punishment, and would tell me to come out into the yard and choose the branch that would be best for flogging me. I was supposed to bring it to him with the bark removed. He would inspect it first, try it out through the air, then tell me to lift my shirt and turn my back toward him. He'd try it on me once or twice and if he wasn't satisfied he would send me to find another one, and promise that the disrespect I showed by choosing the first branch would earn me an even bigger punishment. My father preferred branches from the lemon tree that once stood in our yard. He liked them nice and thick on one end and tapering off on the other. He liked to hold them by the thick part and to hear the noise they made in the air and the noise they made as they hit your body. You weren't allowed to cry, because that would only increase the number of lashes. You weren't allowed to run away, because that could really have ended in catastrophe. You weren't allowed to make him miss. He'd tell me exactly where to stand, to turn a little, to bend over. But I knew then, as I do now, that he did it so we would be the best children in the whole village.

6

oom, boom, boom, boom—the sound reverberates through the whole house. I wake up shrieking uncontrollably and jump out of bed. *Boom, boom, boom*, it continues. It is clearly the sound of shooting, but not the noise I am used to. It is very loud, much louder, the sound of shelling. My wife is on her feet too, and I shout, "The baby, the baby," and the baby begins screaming at the top of her lungs. I hear her screaming and I lie on the floor with my hands above my head. The sound lets up for a minute. "Hurry down," I shout to my wife, and rush into the baby's room. I pick the baby up, hug her in both my arms and try to protect her head. I run down the stairs, and the noise begins again. It's the loudest shelling I've ever heard. I bend over, trying to keep my head hidden, and continue running downstairs. "Into the bathroom," I yell to my wife. "Get into the bathroom." For some reason I figure that is the safest place in the house. At least it's on the lower floor. We go in and I close the door behind me. The baby is screaming and I can't see her face in the dark.

I put the baby into the bathtub. She screams and I bend over her. My palms touch the bathtub floor and my body hovers over her without going beyond the sides of the bathtub itself. It's the safest place to be, I think. My wife is whimpering nearby, on the bathroom floor. She's lying down too. "Put your hands on your head," I tell her.

Another round of shooting, continuous. Judging by the noise, they seem to be shooting at our house, or nearby. Our house is exposed only on its northern side. If the shooting is coming from that direction and not from the roadblock, the bullets will have to go through three walls to reach the bathroom, and to hit me and the baby they'd also have to pierce the bathtub. The baby continues crying and I try to calm her down. "Shhhhh, Baba."

In between rounds I tell my wife to switch with me. She gets into the bathtub and leans over the baby. I lie down on the floor. When the shooting resumes I give off a scream, convinced I've been shot in the back. I try to protect myself by pulling my head toward my legs while lying on my side, with my head toward the bathtub. Another round, then a lull, then another round, and another lull. When the shooting lets up we can hear babies and children and parents shouting in houses nearby. I think of my parents, my older brother, his wife and his little son. Their house is more exposed than ours and it's higher up too. I hope they haven't been hit. I try to concentrate and to make out the voices between rounds, but I can't.

Another round of shooting, and somehow it's less scary than the previous ones. It's amazing what people get used to. Sounds of shooting again, and I wait for a lull, knowing somehow that it will arrive. I try to reassure my wife and daughter.

"It only sounds like it's near, but it's very far away," I say confidently, though it's not what I really think. "They must be shooting at a target," I tell my wife. Her weeping is the only sound in the room. "Shhhh, it will be over any minute, stay down, it's okay, they have nothing to do with us, it's just an echo, they're shooting in a different direction. It will be over soon."

The last lull is much longer. Between the children's crying and the parents' yelling, we can hear the hum of the tank engines not far away. What the hell are they doing? What are they trying to achieve? Who are they shooting at? What's wrong with them? What do they want now? God. We stay in the bathroom even though there's no more shooting. I dare to get up off the floor now, with my arms still covering my head. I stroke my wife's hair. I can feel her trembling. "It's over, you see? That's it. But let's stay here till daybreak. It's not that long."

I lie on my back on the bathroom floor. It's almost completely dark. There's a faint light coming in through the upper window—moonlight, maybe, or tank headlights in the distance. What do they want damn it? Maybe this is just a military drill, or they're just trying to scare us, as if we're not scared enough already? And maybe they've entered the village with their tanks, maybe this was the operation they've been waiting for and now it's behind them. I lie there waiting for the power to come back on too. They must have completed their mission, they must be getting orders to withdraw and put an end to the closure imposed on the village. "Looks to me like it's all over," I tell my wife. "Looks to me like they've finally finished whatever they set out to do, huh? Tomorrow everything will be fine, things will go back to normal."

My heart freezes when I hear the knocking on the front door. I shudder and I can't breathe. I feel my pulse surging all at once and it takes a few seconds before I realize it's only my father at the door. "Is everything okay with you?" he shouts from outside. "Are you okay?" He calls my name. "Yes," I answer him, and try to calm down, taking a deep breath and attempting to overcome the tremors that grip my body. Leaning forward, head first, I feel my way toward the front door, turn the key in the lock and let my father in. "I just wanted to check if everything is okay," he says. "Listen, I was sure they were shooting right here, behind the house."

Where does he get the courage to be outside now? How can he stay so calm? His speech is unchanged, while I do my best to control the quiver in my voice. "Your mother was worried about you, so I came to check. Your brother is fine too. I knocked on their door before. His wife was crying and the boy, poor thing, couldn't stop crying and shaking. I told them to come be with us. You too. Our house is the safest, though it doesn't look like there's going to be any more shooting. Looks like they stopped. In any case, just come over if you're scared. It'll soon be morning anyway."

My father's visit does reassure me. The very thought that you can walk around outside, that they're not shooting at everything within sight of their night-vision binoculars, is comforting. They really aren't interested in ordinary citizens like us. They're looking for specific people. A soldier is a human being, after all, I tell myself, and a human being can't shoot at someone else just like that. There's no chance they'll shoot at random. Nobody wants to kill people for no apparent reason.

My wife would rather we didn't go out at this hour. She wants us to stay home for now. We'll come out of the bathroom, but we'll stay on the bottom floor. I get two blankets from the bedroom. We put the baby on the sofa and cover her. She's fallen back asleep. I sit down beside my wife. Every noise makes us turn to look. I feel her body, which is still shaking, and cover her with a blanket. "That's it, it's over. Stop trembling, I'm telling you, the worst is over. The whole thing is over. Finished."

"You were right. We really did need to look at the whole thing differently. You were right. We really did need to expect the worst."

"There's no point in waiting any longer. I'm telling you, we're through with all that. You'll see, tomorrow we'll have water again, and electricity and the telephone lines will work, and on the news they'll tell the whole story behind this. We'll go back to work, and everything will be okay."

She leans her head on my shoulder. Her warm cheeks make me shiver, and it feels good. For the first time I can feel her seeking reassurance from me, seeing me as a haven for her emotions. For the first time I feel her turning to me for protection. I hold my arm around her shoulder and, like a doting mother, tuck in her blanket. I kiss her tear-stained cheeks. She falls asleep with her head on my shoulder and I stay beside her, feeling the warmth of her body and her breathing on my neck.

189

Sayed Kashua

The darkness changes shades and turns pale, but there's still no light outside. Very slowly I loosen my hold on my wife's shoulder. Gently I move away and let the sofa take the place of the shoulder on which her head was resting. I look for the pack of cigarettes that I left on the dresser. I light one and stand by the window. Apart from the sound of engines in the background, it seems like the dawning of a particularly mild summer's day.

I go into my office on the lower floor and turn on the radio, keeping the volume down, to listen to the six A.M. news. It begins with an item saying that Israeli Arabs from our village had attacked IDF soldiers. It's the first time Israeli Arabs are referred to as terrorists. According to the news, people in our village opened fire on an IDF patrol in the area. "There were no casualties to IDF forces. The soldiers returned fire at those who had fired from within the village."

It's becoming pretty clear to me now that this business is not over. On the contrary, according to the reports, it's getting worse. I find it hard to believe anyone shot at the soldiers. Who in this village could do such a thing? There's nothing organized here, no Hamas, no Jihad, no front of any kind. Maybe soldiers heard an explosion and decided someone was shooting at them, but it's much likelier that the army has concocted this story of a shooting as a good excuse to retaliate. And what about the military patrol they mentioned on the news? And what about the closure? They must have been instructed to use the word *patrol*. Otherwise what would they say? How could they suddenly start talking about roadblocks and closures?

The news reports keep on referring to things being completely peaceful in the cities of the West Bank and Gaza, and to intensive meetings between Israelis and Palestinians. It occurs to me that maybe this lull and those meetings they keep talking about are yet another kind of media double-talk for something altogether different. And why wouldn't they lie about what's happening there if they completely ignore the new reality of our village, and perhaps this applies to all the other Arab villages inside Israel as well? But the few Arab radio stations that I manage to pick up, like Voice of Cairo and Jordanian Radio, also speak of meetings and of calm in the territories. Why would I expect an Arab radio station or an international one to discuss Israeli Arabs? Who are they anyhow?

PART FIVE

The Procession of Armed Men

1

My wife and daughter are still asleep. I decide to make breakfast for my little girl. I'll let my wife sleep it off. There's plenty of powdered milk, I tell myself, enough for a whole week more. I push the cup right under the faucet in the kitchen sink so as not to lose a single drop. I turn it, but all I get is a few drips. Though I'd figured we still had another half tank of water on the roof, there's no water. I climb upstairs, out to the roof and look out over the horizon. The military tanks are still there, surrounded by small figures in green uniforms. I glance at the water tank and discover that the lid has been removed and thrown to the side. I look inside. It's completely empty. Someone has stolen our water. I put my hands to my head. My breathing quickens. From my roof, I can see my brother's and I can tell that the tank on his roof is uncovered too. Those bastards, I'll kill them, those SOBs. Why the hell didn't I think of it? How could I be so careless when things were like this, how could I be such an asshole? There's nothing easier, after all, than climbing up on the roof and stealing water, but who's the SOB who would do such a thing? A strong pain darts through my head. I try to take deep breaths, to get my breathing back to normal, but to no avail. I feel a strong urge to scream as loud as I can. I grit my teeth and, without stopping to think about what's happening to me, I clench my fist and start bashing the empty tank, which responds with a powerful echo.

All of my calculations are off now. But things will be okay, I tell myself. If need be, we'll steal water. The question is where we'll steal it from. Who has any water left? I bet those scumbags climbed up on the roof and could hardly believe their eyes when they saw so much water, the SOBs. They took it all, didn't leave us so much as a drop. I go back down, trying to calm myself, thinking how we can manage with the bottles I bought and hid in the pantry. I count them again. There are five bottles of water and seven of Coke. My parents must have a few more, and I need to find out how many my brother has. This could last us no more than three days. We'll use them for nothing but drinking. The water will be for the children—my brother's and mine. I convince myself that a three-day supply is all we need. If it lasts longer than three more days, other people will starve to death before we do, and it's inconceivable that any army or any country in the world would let people collapse that way, let little children die of thirst and hunger before their very eyes. The commanders must know what things are like in this village, down to the last detail. They know perfectly well that nobody has died of malnutrition yet. They're undoubtedly eyeing the village through their binoculars all the time, and I bet they have their people on the inside, reporting to them about everything that happens. Bastards. I'm sure it's those collaborators who stole our water. They ought to be killed.

I take another bottle of water out of the pantry and pour some of it into the baby's bottle. I won't have any myself. Suddenly I feel a twinge of shame about how I skimped on water but never gave any thought to theft. How could I have overlooked the possibility of theft damn it? Don't I remember where I am? Had I known the water would be stolen, I would at least have had a shower first. I've never been so filthy and smelly in my life.

The baby's bottle is ready. I leave it on the counter and have another cigarette by the window. It's still early in the morning, and people are in no hurry to leave their homes. You can hear the crying of babies in the homes nearby. My parents must be awake by now, but I'll wait till my wife and daughter wake up and then we'll join them. The baby is the first to wake up. I lift her off the sofa, hug her, say good morning in the tone that she's grown used to. I wonder if she's aware of what's going on around her. I put the bottle to her lips and she clasps it tightly and starts drinking. Ever since she was born, I've been worrying. In the early months I worried about crib death, about unexpected reactions to inoculations, about road accidents, about childhood illnesses. Sometimes I'd wake up in a panic and go check if she was still breathing. It never occurred to me that I'd actually have to worry about her having enough to eat. I never imagined a moment when I'd picture my little girl starving to death or lying on her bed bleeding after a bullet hit her.

Scenes of children killed in the Intifada run through my mind. I think of the funerals and the posters of Palestinian babies who'd had half their skulls shot off, or photographs taken at hospitals, of babies with blood-soaked diapers, babies who had died and looked as if they were just asleep. Israeli TV doesn't actually show pictures of dead Jewish babies. They make do with pictures of the child when he or she was still alive. I hold my daughter tight, clutching her. The sound of her sucking on her bottle intensifies my fears. It's the first time I feel hopeless. Because until now, despite all we've been through, I knew I'd manage somehow and one way or another I'd figure out a way for my loved ones and myself to survive.

My wife wakes up and turns her head nervously till she sees me and the baby. "What happened?" she asks, concerned. "Everything's okay," I quickly reassure her. I move closer and finger her hair, hoping she still wants my support. She bows her head, trying to sort out what has happened to her during the night and to figure out how much of it was reality and how much a dream. She takes the baby from me, with the bottle still in her mouth, places her in her lap and asks, "Was there any more shooting after I fell asleep? Have they left?" I shrug. "No, they didn't shoot any more after that. I don't know if they've left," I lie. "I haven't gone outdoors yet. We'll go over to my parents' soon and find out what's going on. But I don't think there's going to be any school today."

2

There is nobody in the streets except the Palestinian workers. The mayor and villagers have ordered them to collect the garbage and dispose of it in the soccer field at the outskirts of the village. People are in no hurry to leave their homes this morning. They're suspicious, still unable to figure out what exactly was happening during the night and what the shooting was all about. The Palestinians are the only ones still working. Some of them see us making our way to our parents' home and make a sign for *food* by putting their hands to their mouths. I ignore their gestures, not because I don't care but because I don't want to give the impression that we have any food left. I shrug as if to indicate I wished I had some. My parents' house looks dirtier than usual. There are spots on the floor despite my mother's attempts to get rid of them with a dry rag. The fact that their tank would run dry before ours was to be expected. Their home has always been the place where everyone congregated and where everything happened, a kind of extended-family living room. We ate most of our meals there even before all this began, and Mother was never one to skimp on food or water. But my calculations were off and in fact somehow the faucets in my parents' home remain the last ones from which we can still squeeze a few glasses of water.

"Do you believe it? They've stolen our water," my brother greets me. "They climbed up on my roof and yours and stole the water." He tells me this as if it were new to me. For him it is yet another thing to tell, and he is very agitated as he says it—more agitated to be standing there and telling me such things than he is at the implications of his report. I nod and look at my wife, who is becoming even more anxious. "It isn't so terrible," I reply at once, but I'm actually thinking of my wife as I say it. "I bought a few bottles of drinks that should last us quite a while. I promise you that even though they've stolen our water, we'll be the last ones in the village to run out. By then everything will be okay."

My response has a mildly calming effect on them all, though I've allowed myself a deliberate overstatement. I explain that from now on, water will be used for nothing but drinking, and it should be for the children only. We'll manage on fruit juice or carbonated drinks. "No more cooking with water," I tell my mother. "And let's not even think of tea or coffee. One thing's for sure: we've got to guard whatever food and water we have left against thieves. I suggest we bring everything we have and put it here, at Mother and Father's house, the only place that always has people in it. The safest place for the important things is right here."

My two brothers join me. We begin at my house. I get a few large plastic garbage bags to use for moving the food. "We don't want anyone to see what we're moving," I say. At first they laugh at the quantities of food I've bought, the bags of rice and flour and the canned goods. There isn't much we can do with the rice and flour without water anyway, so we only take the drinks, the baby food and the cans. There was less than I'd expected in my older brother's house. He had no drinks left at all. Mostly he had potatoes, wafers and candy bars.

3

There's the sound of heavy shooting again, but not the same as last night, and there's lots of noise in the next street. As we all duck and the women start screaming, Father goes outside, unperturbed, to see what's going on. "It's just shooting," he says. "Some local guys shooting in the air. Come see for yourselves." My brother and I go out, and the women and children stay indoors. A large group, several dozen men, their faces covered in blue-and-red checkered kaffiyehs, are making their way down the road with their weapons held high. Every once in a while one of the men presses the trigger, letting loose a round of shots. A group of children are following them along, some dragging their bikes, trying to get close enough to inspect the weapons. Every time one of the guys shoots, the children cheer.

The next-door neighbors come out too and stand in their doorways to watch the show, a first for us. They gather around, and we join them. Some of them already know that the young men from the village have shot at the soldiers. A few of the neighbors are saying the guys actually managed to kill some soldiers at the roadblock and that this accounted

202

for all the shooting during the previous night. They hit a few houses, but nobody in the village was killed. The younger children say they've already seen the houses that were hit, that the bullets were enormous and made holes through the walls of the buildings they hurt, and that it's a miracle nobody was hit.

A few of the older women shout with joy at the sight of the armed men, as if they were warriors about to liberate the village from a siege. The young men's face coverings are not enough to conceal their identities. On the contrary—they are all well known and are recognized in no time. All of them have a criminal record, they are members of a gang that steals cars and pushes drugs, the kind of gang that have become an inseparable part of the local scene. Now the women are shouting and treating them like war heroes. Their attempt at imitating well-known Palestinian scenes is pathetic. What can they be thinking? And just what organization do they belong to? The pitiful scene of drug dealers and thieves roaming the village streets like some kind of new heroes can only mean bad news. They are being joined by more and more people ostensibly wanting to be part of the victory march, following them, showing support and cheering. The villagers seem to have decided on a new form of leadership, headed by criminals who acquired their weapons for illegal purposes, definitely not nationalistic ones. What exactly does the nationalist consciousness of those people consist of? Not that this matters anymore. They've got their weapons, they've got a hold on the village and now everyone is supposed to cheer and salute them.

The neighbors go on standing in the road, trying to find somewhere not covered with sewage, and follow the procession till it disappears out of sight. They name the gang members they've recognized. Some of them think the idea of turning into mujahideen overnight laughable, others are all in favor and say that maybe this way the army will withdraw. They go on to discuss events of the previous night, the enormous panic caused by the shooting, how they thought we were being overrun by tanks and helicopters.

"Let's just hope they don't shoot again tonight. I want the children to get some sleep," one of them says.

"First you'll have to persuade the new fighters not to shoot. Who is their leader anyway?"

"Why shouldn't they shoot? At least to hit them, to make them suffer a little. What they're doing to us is bad enough. We have nothing left to feed the children. Just stale bread, and no water at all. How much longer are we going to put up with it?"

"It's the mayor's responsibility. I bet his house is packed with food."

"What do they want anyway? If they don't reconnect the water today and let in some food, we're going to starve to death. What's going on here? Where are our members of the Knesset? Where are the left-wingers? This is the fourth day, and nobody is saying a thing. What are they trying to do, kill us by dehydration? Even on the West Bank they never did that."

"But if armed people are shooting at the soldiers, it's only going to make things more complicated. And if they were planning to stop this thing today, it's going to take a few more days now."

"What do you mean, a few more days? We don't have a few more days. Half the village will starve to death by then. What, are they crazy? What do you mean, a few more days?"

4

The armed procession develops into a riot. The children and teens who haven't joined hang around, and soon all hell breaks loose. They've begun to act like anything goes, as if the law, which had remained a deterrent even when the law enforcers had stopped entering the village, no longer exists. Groups of residents, especially the younger ones, break into the bank—not that there is any money left, according to my brother—destroy equipment and set fire to everything. The same thing happens at the post office. At all of the government-run institutions in the village, in fact. They even set fire to the health-fund clinic, though it's no longer in operation. Once they ran out of medication, it closed down. The doctors see their patients at home, asking to be paid in food, mostly, or else demanding exorbitant sums of money or valuable jewelry. Stories are already circulating about the parents who handed over a gold ring in return for a suppository to get their baby's fever down. The thugs vent their rage at the large shops too. There is no food left, but they take off with appliances, toilet paper and cosmetics. It seems like there's no chance things will ever return to normal. True, these are small groups, by no means the whole population, but that's all it takes to create an atmosphere of utter chaos which will be difficult to eliminate even when the whole business is over and done with.

The soldiers aren't reacting at all, and the villagers themselves seem to forget about the possibility of being shot at. The soldiers who have weapons feel free to brandish them as if they're shooting on the village. If it does happen again, it will only be at night, as if there are rules to separate things that are done in broad daylight from things that are done behind a veil of darkness. It stands to reason that if the thugs decide to push their luck again and start to provoke the soldiers, it will only happen in the darkness, and they won't risk shooting while they are so exposed.

Every now and then I go outside and look at the sections of the village that stretch across from my parents' home as far as I can see. There is black smoke rising in a few places, and lots of people roaming about aimlessly, undeterred by the filth, the rivulets of sewage and the endless swarms of flies.

My father and two brothers decide to go into the town, to check things out, or so they say. I consider joining them but my wife looks at me, her expression a plea not to leave her on her own. "I want us to go to my parents', to see how they're doing," she says, looking exhausted and drawn. "I'd like you to drive me there, please."

We get into the car. She doesn't fasten the baby's seat belt the way she always does but holds her in her lap and sits next to me in the front seat. Suddenly the car seems like a bubble from another world. I turn on the air conditioner and the radio too, looking for a station that plays music, and the whole car, with a pleasant fragrance lingering inside it, becomes an island of sanity, giving both of us, my wife and myself, a whiff of our lives before the current situation. The trip in the air-conditioned car makes us forget our sorrow over the present reality and gives me some hope. It reminds me that my life normally looks very different from what it has looked like over the past few days. I learn to appreciate it now and hope it goes back to what it was very soon. For a few minutes there's also the hope, which I'd already begun to consider a delusion, that everything will blow over soon and things will go back to the way they were. I try to convince myself to treat all the events of the past few days like a story, a major spread that will win me back my position at the paper and put me in my rightful place on the front pages. "What are you so worried about?" I ask my wife, and even manage a smile. "Things will be okay. Listen to the radio. They're playing music. Everything's fine."

"Now I'm the one who's worried and you're the one who's calm. How do you explain that? Earlier, when you were panicking, everyone thought you were crazy, and now, when everyone's on edge, you behave as if nothing's wrong?"

"What could be wrong? They're not out to destroy us, or else they could have done that within hours. I promise you the gag order will be lifted soon and we'll find out what made them do it. I'm sure it's something really trivial and we'll all wind up laughing about it."

"My gut feeling is that things are going to be bad, nothing is going to be the way it was before."

I know, I think, nothing is going to be the way it was. That's for sure. But what's the point of adding to my wife's worries now? She looks at the kids roaming the streets, watching the last traces of the fires outside the public buildings and the stores. The eyes of the children don't seem to reflect any fear, which is more than I can say about the adults. They're bound to be hungry and thirsty, but I guess that children like these, who spend most of their time in the streets, see any new situation as cause for celebration. It's as if their current setting is better suited to them than the seemingly peaceful lives they led in the village until recently. You can see them deep in conversation or having an argument, trying to outdo one another in the number of fires they'd seen or the number of spent shells they'd found from soldiers and criminals. They show off their collections and take special pride in the larger specimens, those from the soldiers. Some of the kids are riding their bikes barefoot, trying to keep up with the car, holding on to the handlebars with one hand and displaying their bullets in the other. Smiling, they let me and every passerby see their loot. Who knows, maybe they're the ones who stole the water from our tank.

Getting to my wife's parents' home isn't easy. The main road is blocked. People in this stinking village prefer to keep driving to the last drop of gas. They couldn't care less that they'll wind up leaving their car in the middle of the road, blocking it.

As far as they're concerned, if they can't go anywhere, then neither should anyone else. Then again, a few of the drivers who have run out of gas have gone to the trouble of pushing their cars to the side of the road, and the side street leading to my wife's parents' home isn't blocked. Ever so slowly I manage to wend my way between the cars scattered along the road. It's incredible how inconsiderate people can be sometimes.

5

My wife and mother-in-law burst into tears when they see each other. They hug each other tightly and sob. My father-in-law paces nervously and mutters, "What good is that going to do, what's the point of crying now?" Ashraf comes out of his room, looking very tired. He hasn't shaven in days. He tries to give his usual smile but it looks different now. I've never seen him this way. He shakes my hand and asks, in Hebrew as usual, "What's up, Uncle?" Then he asks if I've got a cigarette, and I can tell how uncomfortable he is having to ask.

"Yes," I say, and pull out a pack that's almost full. "I've got plenty of cigarettes. I guess it's the only thing I won't be short of," I say in an attempt to make him feel better about it. I want to make sure he's not embarrassed, because I really do have enough.

My wife and her parents are sitting on mattresses on the living room floor, discussing the events of the past few days. Ashraf and I go outside. We sit on the steps and smoke our cigarettes. He looks shattered, which isn't too surprising.

"Don't worry," I tell him. "Things will work out okay."

He watches me exhale and breaks into tears. It's the first time I've seen him cry. "What's going to work out okay? They must have brought in someone to replace me in the phone company by now," he says. "It took me forever to find that job and now, just like that, because of something that has nothing to do with me, I'll lose it." He wipes away his tears. I know how hard it was for him to find that job after he graduated from the university, and that he couldn't find anything in his field. Far from it. Customer service doesn't require any education, but I can still remember how happy he and his family were when he finally found it. To tell the truth, I was kind of surprised that in our situation a person would still be thinking about the problem of losing a job. People barely have enough to drink. Every trace of a normal modern life has disappeared, and here he is, crying over the possibility that he may have lost a job that had paid him minimum wage.

"It's all because of those sons of bitches," he says. "I'm telling you, it's all because of those thugs who're walking around waving their Uzis like heroes. I know a lot of people think what the Israelis are doing to this village is on account of the Islamic Movement or terrorists who are hiding out here, but that's bullshit. What the government is looking for are gangs. They've figured out that there are more weapons in this village than in the entire West Bank. It's probably beginning to get to them by now, because the gangs have begun selling weapons to the Hamas. The government used to do everything possible to make sure that everything involving crime or drugs or weapons and every kind of shit the country had to offer would stay in the

Arab villages, and now they've realized it's gotten out of control. They gave them free rein, not a single damn cop came into the village. You could call the police and report a dead body in your backyard and it would take them five hours to get there, after they'd made sure it wasn't dangerous and that there was no chance anyone would object. Now they know that only the army and the tanks and roadblocks can solve the problem.

"Now they understand, the sons of bitches, that what they've created here is more dangerous than any Palestinian or Muslim organization that exists. All they want is for the gangs to hand over their weapons. They won't dare come into the village because they know how much ammunition we have here. Some of the criminals have LAU missiles. The army won't come in. They'll wait for those guys to surrender. The problem is that by the time this happens, our lives will be completely ruined. Not that the gang members will run short of food or water. They just barge into people's houses and take whatever they want. They have a whole army of flunkies who get hold of food for them. Now they're God. The truth is that they've always been God."

Ashraf stops for a minute and takes a puff on his cigarette. My mother-in-law asks if I'd like something to drink. "No," I say. "No, thanks." I don't know what the supplies situation is like in my wife's parents' house and I know she's only asking to be polite, because normally they would just serve something without asking. I look at Ashraf. He's scratching his head; his eyes are still puffy. "I don't know," I say. "Doesn't it seem like too much, all on account of a few criminals?"

213

"A few criminals," he mocks me. "You've got no idea what goes on around here. This whole village is one big crime district. Who do you think calls the shots here, huh? The religious leaders? The mayor?" He sniggers. "You have no idea what goes on, because you don't have the real picture of how things work. It's all about power, about who has more weapons and more men. Did you know that all of the gambling joints in Israel are controlled by Arabs? Did you know that every Arab region is in charge of a Jewish one? Who do you think controls the prostitution, the casinos and the money changing and anything you can think of in Tel Aviv or Kfar Sava, huh? Who? The police? They run the protection business in the entire area and God help anyone who messes with them or refuses to pay them protection money. Now the state is beginning to think about it, now that they're tripping all over us in their cities. People like Bassel scare them more than Bin Laden, believe me."

Ashraf's words send a chill up my spine. It's not that I think he's right. On the contrary, I think he's wrong, in a big way. He's always been prone to exaggeration when it comes to the power of the gangs. From the little I managed to get out of him since my return, I've learned enough to know that the crime situation really is bad and that most people are living in constant fear of the gangs, but still, it wasn't a situation that would lead to a military operation like this. No way. The thing that scared me most in the whole story was when he mentioned Bassel. "Who's this Bassel?" I ask him.

"He's the strongest person in the village right now. You know him. He's your age," Ashraf says, and adds Bassel's family name. "Believe me, if anyone is negotiating with the police or the army about this whole situation, it's bound to be him and not the mayor."

6

The village is completely still. The heavy midday heat has chased everyone indoors. Like us, most people must have discovered that the best way to avoid hunger and thirst is to take a nap. In our house everyone's sprawled out, whether on the beds or on mattresses on the floor. My younger brother and I chose the living room sofas. Apart from the two small children, nobody is sleeping. Everyone seems to be deep in thought about the situation but prefers not to discuss it with the others. What good could it do to share our concerns? I try to think of ways of getting hold of more water. The use of force won't help when it comes to a family that has no record of fights or violence. I wonder what would happen if we dug some water holes in the village. Maybe the groundwater would rise to the surface and give enough not only for us but for everyone. And maybe there are pipes running under our land, leading from the reservoirs and the rivers of the Galilee to the cities in the center and the desert in the south. If people here could get their act together, maybe they could still come up with a constructive idea for the water supply. Obviously it won't be enough to have just one person or one family digging. There has to be full cooperation. Except that nothing could cause the villagers to cooperate now. They'll only go for a quick fix. I hope the ones who stole our water die of poisoning!

Food is less of a problem than water. True, there's hardly any land left in the village to plant things on—crops that could give us something to eat—but for now, we haven't run out yet, and maybe we could hunt birds. In my mind's eye I see scenes of our childhood—mine and my brothers'. We spent whole days trying to catch pigeons and other birds, using a box, a stick and a piece of string. All you needed was some patience. I try to take my mind off the food, I try not to think about water, because it only makes me thirstier. Actually I've had nothing to drink since last night. Everyone else has had one glass but I decided to do without, like a kind of model of sacrifice. Not that anyone paid special attention to me. Luckily, I still have some cigarettes, the only thing I don't skimp on because I know very well that everything else will run out long before the cigarettes do. And what's the good of having cigarettes when you've got no water?

I get up slowly, take the pack of cigarettes and go outside to have one. My younger brother sees me and gets up too without making a sound. The two of us light up. He's much less scared of my father now. "If he catches me smoking out here, I'll tell him I just started because people told me it makes you forget your hunger and thirst," he quips, and I don't say a word.

"What do you think?" my brother begins, and I nod and feel my whiskers with my left hand. "I don't know, but it's got to end. It can't go on for even one more day."

"What are they saying on the radio? You do still listen to the news, don't you?"

"They aren't saying anything. Judging by all the panels and the experts talking about Israeli Arabs, it's obvious that there's a big problem, because they keep referring to us as a threat, as something that calls for a solution, but they haven't said anything about what's happening."

"Tell me, are they interviewing any Arabs?"

"Not a single one. Which is scary too. And it seems like everyone is in the same boat, not just our village."

"What, even the MKs and the mayors?"

"Not a single Arab is being interviewed. Nothing. It must have something to do with the new security orders. Besides, maybe they can't get hold of us. How can they get hold of the mayor? No chance."

"Strange. The defense minister's supposed to be a friend of his, isn't he? How many plates of hummus did they share?" my brother asks.

"Yes, but if this is everybody's problem, maybe it's a good sign. I mean, they can't keep all the Arab villages in this condition much longer. They're certainly not planning to starve everyone to death. Something enormous must have happened."

"What? Israeli Arabs got control of the Defense Ministry?"

"Something like that."

"And maybe someone from our village is holding the prime minister hostage with a knife and they're holding on to all of us till he's released," my brother says with a laugh, and this time I laugh too.

"All I know is I've lost a year of school," he says.

"Don't worry," I say. "They'll schedule a special make-up exam for the Arabs."

7

My younger brother and I sit on the front steps and look out over the village, which is waking up with a start. The midday nap has run its course, and everyone's back on their feet. All at once, as if an alarm bell has rung, the streets are crowded. First the children and then the adults. The children are hungry. Luckily for our two, we still have some food left and they don't feel the shortages the way we do. My wife goes outside carrying the baby and shaking a bottle of formula. I restrain myself, trying not to scream at her for doing something so stupid. I whisper softly in her ear that we don't want the whole world to know we have baby formula left. As if she's suddenly grasped a very deep idea, she rushes back inside. But it's too late. A neighbor has seen her and rushes over to where we're sitting outdoors. "I beg you, I have nothing to give my children. Please let me have some milk."

"We have barely half a carton left," I lie to her. "Not enough for the baby for even one more day."

"Please, just two tablespoons," she says. "For my little one. She's starving."

A crowd is gathering at the entrance to our house, watching the drama unfold. "We don't have any," I tell her. "I wish we did." I speak louder to make sure they can all hear me. I know perfectly well that if I give her any, even a small amount, if won't end there. Everyone's going to want some. "You don't understand." By now I'm shouting. "Leave us alone. You're the last thing we need now." But she persists. The short, overweight neighbor who never visited us—and we never visited her either—is suddenly convinced that we owe it to her to give her some food. It isn't a request anymore, it's a demand, a right we're depriving her of. "But I saw you had food," she yells, well aware that everyone is listening. "If I hadn't seen it, I might believe you."

"And I'm telling you this is all we have. Our daughter has nothing left after this bottle."

Now my entire family joins me outside, except for my wife—the one who's really to blame for this new development, but I can't really take it out on her. "What do you want?" my father intervenes now. "Go away. What is this, a public spectacle?"

"Give her some milk," someone in the crowd shouts, and I recognize the voice of the polite grocery store owner, whom we've known for many years. "You bought out half the store yourself," he yells, and the neighbor confronting us draws strength from this reinforcement. She looks determined, with no intention of leaving before her demand is met. Her eyes are mean, and I get the feeling that her real aim isn't so much to feed her children as to increase her supply of food. Hungry children cry, and we haven't heard any of hers crying yet.

Dozens of people are standing around, waiting for the show to run its course. The neighbor yells something that we can't make out, curses and tries to force her way into our house. "I'll get it myself," she yells. I grab her fat body and try to stop her. She's very strong and I have a hard time restraining her.

"Get the hell out of here, you lunatic," I shout, and push her backward, but she tries again. More people are approaching the door now, trying to get in as well. My heart is pounding. My brothers block the entrance as the number of trespassers grows. I can't keep them out and they're going to break into the house. I feel stifled and flushed. With one hand, I push away the ugly neighbor and hate her more than anything in the world. And I think about my wife and how I'm going to let her have it later. I clench my fist, lower my right hand and shove it as hard as I can into the neighbor's stomach. She recoils in pain, grasping her middle. I can hear myself scream.

Mother gets behind us, cursing at the top of her lungs and brandishing a broomstick. I take it from her and use it to push away anyone who comes near us. I would never have thought myself capable of using such force. I've never had to be violent before. I push children down on the ground. I force my way to the front, leaving my brothers behind, and charge at the crowd, which keeps growing, though only a few of them actually try to get inside the house. I wave the stick at them and shout, "I'll kill you. I'll bury anyone who tries to get any closer." And I pounce on them with the stick. It deters them a bit and they retreat. "Get out of here, you dogs. We have nothing. You should be ashamed of yourselves."

Now my younger brother comes out and takes his place by my side with a spade in his hand, threatening to hit anyone who dares come closer. Some of the people start throwing stones at us and at the house. One of the stones hits me in the hand, and I stand there in a puddle of sewage feeling the pain in my hand and watching the stones fly in our direction. I know I have nothing to lose. Not that I have much time to think, but instead of the stones scaring me they only make me more angry and I run toward the stone-throwers, with my brother close behind. I yell as loud as I can and smash the broomstick down on the back of a little boy, who falls into the sewage. The others retreat, but the barrage of stones grows stronger and they're hitting me all over, but that doesn't stop me either. One of the stones hits me right in the mouth, and I lunge ahead.

A heavy round of shots causes everyone to stop. The people facing the house bend over and put their hands to their ears. They're no longer throwing stones. I turn my head and see that my brothers are bending over and covering their ears too. I'm the only one still standing there, with my stick, breathing heavily, my chest rising and falling faster than ever and the blood dripping from my mouth onto my shirt. Two of the armed thugs from the morning's victory march form a barrier between me and the crowd. They wave their weapons high in the air and shout, "What's going on here? Enough!" And the crowd, ready to obey the new forces in control, shout out, "They have food."

One of the armed guys, who'll never miss a chance to fire, lets loose another round, and the other one shouts, "Quiet." The one who appears to be their leader asks me what happened, and I explain that they tried to break into our house because they thought we had food. I calm down and speak to him with the respect due to a new master. I find I talk more simply in the hope that he'll understand me better. "They have no shame, trying to break into a house full of women and children. My wife is inside, trying to feed our baby to get her to stop crying, and these people just break in. They have no consideration." I know that to our new leaders shows of respect and honor are very important. "People have no shame anymore," my father adds from behind me.

"They have food," the grocery store owner shouts again. He's facing them now. "The guy you're talking to bought out half my store. He knew before everyone that there would be a war. People at his newspaper must have told him." I shake my head. "I got ready just like everyone else," I say quietly to the armed guy facing me, who has no idea what to do but still feels obliged to impose order. He's even enjoying it. "If you do have food, you've got to share some of it," he says. "People are starving to death. Give away some of it, okay?"

"Okay," I say, and put down my stick. I realize I have no choice. There have already been break-ins at the homes of people who are considered wealthy. We're not in that category, of course, but nothing is going to stop these people, who are convinced we lack for nothing. "All right," I say again, speaking louder. "There isn't a single piece of bread in my parents' house. It's all in my house."

As soon as they hear this, the crowd starts running as fast as they can toward the new houses behind my parents'. The two men shooting in the air don't deter them this time and they break into a wild gallop, bending over but continuing the race for the loot. The armed men follow, trying to get things under control. I turn around and, looking at my family, I see how sorry they're feeling for me. We hear the sound of the door breaking, which doesn't disturb us too much. Children and adults run out with big smiles on their faces, carrying sacks of rice, sugar, salt, coffee and flour. They break into my brother's house too, but don't find as much. We don't need any of those things. Whatever we could use we moved to my parents' house in the morning. I sit down on the front steps and look at the people. Most of them I recognize. They're from our neighborhood, after all, some of them close neighbors. The commotion soon dies out, and everyone moves away, probably looking for the next arena. The two armed men come back to me. "I'm sorry," the leader says. "We wanted you to share some of it, but they got it all. Don't worry, I know the ones who took it, and we'll bring some of it back. You have my word. And we made sure they didn't take any of the furniture or appliances. The only thing they took is food. Don't worry, we'll be back."

I stay sitting there on the steps. In our house we know we won. My brothers and father go to check out the new houses. I go inside and wipe off the blood with a dry piece of paper. My wife brings me a glass of water. I drink half of it and hand it back to her. I go into my boyhood room and lie down, my face in the pillow. My body is trembling and my face is on fire. I shut my eyes and cry in silence.

8

My mother comes in. I manage to open my eyes just slightly and see her through my wet eyelashes. She leaves the room and whispers, "He's asleep," then shuts the door behind her.

I lie on my bed and think of my mother, picture her as if she were a little girl before a class trip. Then I think of her rushing about in the kitchen, preparing sandwiches, wrapping them in silver foil. The sandwiches are my father's favorite, with fried ground meat and pickles, sliced lengthwise. He won't touch them if she slices them the usual way, four such sandwiches for him and two for her, with cheese. She'll eat whatever there is. It's food for the trip. She rushes about, wearing a colored scarf on her head, sweating, short and fat. When I was a child, I hated how my mother looked. It took me a long time to realize she was considered a pretty woman. She still is, for her age.

In my daydream my brothers are asleep by now, but I can't doze off. I could never fall asleep on days when my parents went away for their regular ten-day vacation. Always ten days, always in July, sometimes to Turkey, sometimes to Eilat, or Sinai or Egypt, and lately to Jordan too. It happens every year, and I just can't get used to it. In fact, it gets worse as the years go by. I stand there in silence, leaning against one of the kitchen walls, and watch her. She's preparing coffee. In a moment, she'll be pouring it into a thermos bottle, because my father can't last half an hour without his extra bitter coffee, with no sugar.

It's late, and my father went to bed long ago. Their suitcase is packed and soon their food will be packed too. All my mother has left to do is to fill a few bottles with water and put them in the freezer. They'll be frozen by the time she and my father leave, and the cold water will last all the way to Cairo. She finishes, takes another look in the fridge, counts the sandwiches and mutters to herself as she tries to make sure she hasn't forgotten anything. The bus will be arriving soon, and they'll be leaving at five A.M. She has just two hours left. Everything's ready.

"Come on, get into bed," she tells me, taking off her scarf and using it to wipe the perspiration from her face and forehead. How I hate that gesture of hers. My mother doesn't care about me. I'm convinced of it. Mother never understands what I am going through. If she did, she'd never have go and leave me home alone. When I told her earlier in the evening that I didn't feel sleepy, because I'd slept a lot in the afternoon, she believed me, and when I say good night to her now and head for the children's room, she's sure I'm going to sleep. My mother isn't the kind of mother who tucks her children into bed at night. She keeps saying she can't understand women who are sad that they're childless, and that only crazy women have children. My mother brought three children into the world and she keeps telling her girlfriends and us that it's too many. My

227

mother doesn't love us. At least she has never told any of us that she loves us. Sometimes I think my brothers have no problem with it, because they seem pretty happy. For me, having a mother who hates us is tough, but I never mention it to anybody.

I stay awake. I know Mother is still awake too. How she loves these trips. She keeps telling people that without these annual trips she'd collapse. She works like a dog all year and then come the ten days without dishes, without cooking and especially without children. I hear her get into the bathtub to bathe and I picture her fat body with all the soap and water. My father wakes up half an hour later and he too begins to get dressed. They talk quietly, in order not to wake anyone. I can't hear what they're saying. I wait another few minutes, wipe away my tears and get up to go to the kitchen. Soon they'll be leaving. I say good morning and they don't reply. They're checking their papers and their passports. "Go wait outside," Father says. "Watch the bags, and call us when the bus gets here."

I sit on the steps next to their bags. Dawn is breaking, and it's a little chilly even though it's summertime. The hair on the back of my hand bristles and I enjoy the feel of the goose bumps on my skin.

What could possibly happen? I ask myself, and try not to answer the question. They go away every year and in the end they come back. I struggle not to think all the bad thoughts that race through my mind, because I know that if I do, they'll probably come true. I know for sure that if anything bad happens to my parents, it will always be because of me. I have to think positive. I'll try to concentrate on the presents they'll bring me. I bet they'll bring me sneakers and maybe this time they'll get the right size.

I see the bus coming up the road and I call out like the happiest kid in the world, "The bus is here." My parents, who are all ready, rush outside, as though if they're a second late, the bus will leave without them. My father carries the large suitcase, my mother takes the lunch bag and I follow with a container of water covered in Styrofoam, which I carry with both hands. They put everything into the luggage compartment of the bus, except for the water, the coffee and the little bag that Mother carries on her shoulder. Most of the passengers are adults but a few have brought along a child or two. My parents get into the bus, sit by the window nearest me, look at me and don't say a word. They don't even wave good-bye and I don't wave to them either. The bus begins to pull out. I wait for it to disappear in the direction it came from and only then can I relax my muscles and let my body tremble.

I have ten days of waiting ahead of me now. I always remind myself that it's only nine nights. The nights are the main problem. I pull out the chart I've prepared, of the days and the nights, and allow myself to tick off the first day even though it hasn't begun yet. Grandmother will be arriving soon, as she does every year, bringing Grandfather with her. They'll stay for ten days and nine nights.

She arrives before my brothers wake up, just as she does every year. They live not far from us, a five-minute walk away. If their house were larger, my mother would send us to stay with them, but they live in a single room. The rest of the house is used by my only uncle, my mother's brother. My grandmother arrives early because she doesn't want people to see her carrying Grandfather on her shoulder. She is old, she looks about a hundred years old, but she's still strong and my grandfather is light as a small child. My grandmother is perspiring. She puts Grandfather down on the bed in my parents' bedroom in his regular position, lying on his back, staring at the ceiling. My grandfather never gets out of bed by himself. He doesn't move at all. For as long as I've known him, he's been in this position, just lying on his back. My parents keep saying what a strong man he was before his illness. They say he was the richest man in the village, the best salesman, the first man to buy a car and to build a fancy stone house. But we never knew him like that. Sometimes my parents tell us how he lay in bed after he returned from the pilgrimage to Mecca. They say that right there, in the middle of town, in front of everyone, a thief was beheaded, because that's how it is in Islam and it scared us out of our wits and we never stole anything ever. They say the sight of it destroyed him completely, and that he was a different person after that.

I like looking at my grandfather. I like how thin he is and how his face is so small, his cheeks so shriveled, his mouth so wide open and his eyes protruding and staring at the ceiling. People kept saying he was going to die, but that was many years ago, and he hasn't died. My mother used to say that sometimes if God loves him and us both, He ought to take him. She was waiting for him to die, and I couldn't understand how anyone could want a father to die. So what if he lay in bed all the time? My grandmother bends over, holds her waist with one hand, mumbles something about how heavy he is and that she's turning into an old lady. She sits down for a minute on the living room sofa, but then gets up and goes into the kitchen, looking for the pots and pans, checking the fridge, taking out tomatoes and eggs and getting breakfast started.

My grandmother doesn't hear a word. It's not because of her age. She never did hear anything. She can speak and when you get used to it, you can understand what she wants. My parents say her problem can be treated and that there are all kinds of gadgets in the Jewish hospitals, but my grandmother doesn't want that. She says she doesn't need it and that what she hears is too much as it is.

I'm so jealous of my brothers. They don't care that our parents are gone. On the contrary, sometimes it seems as if our parents' absence makes them happier. They can play the whole time, they can go to bed whenever they want and they say Grandmother makes wonderful food, that her enormous breakfast gives us lots of choices, not like what Mother fixes, only one thing. They always laugh at Grandfather and when Grandmother is not around my older brother gets a stick and pokes at him. Sometimes he pokes it into Grandfather's mouth and nose and he cracks up when Grandfather doesn't react.

My grandmother works all the time, even though there isn't that much to do. Either she's preparing something in the kitchen or else she's cleaning or she's taking care of Grandfather. She brings him yogurt, mixes it and forces it into him, a spoonful at a time. Sometimes it drips out and she wipes his mouth and mutters things. I can't tell if she's muttering to herself or to him. Sometimes she carries him on her shoulder, takes him to the bathroom, puts him back in my parents' bed or else on the sofa and goes outside to hang wet pieces of white cloth on the laundry line. In the mornings she takes him outside and puts him on a mattress in the sun. Then at noon she takes him back to bed and in the afternoon, back to the mattress outside.

I get through the days somehow, playing with my brothers and with the kids from the neighborhood. Nights are a problem, though. But my grandfather helps me a lot. My grandmother never sleeps next to him, and my two brothers won't do it either because they say he smells awful. I'm glad Grandmother sleeps in my bed so I can sleep next to Grandfather, and take comfort from the fact that an adult is lying next to me, awake. My grandfather never shuts his eyes, and that's very good. And despite his strong smell, I can feel the ever-so-familiar scent of my parents in that bed. Before I climb into it, I make sure to tick off another night that's passed. It's dark and I'll be asleep anyway and then it will be tomorrow, even though I can hardly close my eyes and I cry almost every night.

I wonder if anything bad will happen to them. If it does, how long will it be before we know about it? How long does it take for news to travel from Cairo to our home? The thought that they could be dead and we won't know it drives me crazy. I keep picturing an overturned bus and two bodies. I always run toward Father's body, only Father's. My fears are always about Father. I never dwell on the possibility of something bad happening to my mother. As far as I'm concerned, it's okay if she dies.

On nights when I can't fall asleep, I tell Grandfather everything. Not out loud but in a whisper, right into his ear. All the bad things I see I tell him, and then I feel better. I tell him how when anyone in the family dies someone always bangs hard on the door, and how scared I am when my parents go out. I tell him how I saw the bodies of my two uncles in coffins and that I couldn't fall asleep afterward, how I'm convinced my father will go to hell because he doesn't do any of the things that the religion teacher says you have to do, that I know I'll go to heaven and my father won't. My grandfather continues to stare up at the ceiling and sometimes I cover him and ask, "Are you warm enough?" or "Are you cold?" and he doesn't answer.

Before going to sleep on the last night, I don't tick off the final day. I'll wait for the following morning to do that. If they set out from Cairo at the same time as they set out from here, five A.M., they ought to be here by five P.M. I do whatever I can to fall asleep, to get the time to pass quickly. I tell Grandfather all my stories from the beginning, shut my eyes tight and think about nice things, but nothing works. I don't fall asleep for a minute, because bad things always happen in the end, just when you're expecting something nice, and what could be better than to have my parents back? What could possibly be better than to see my father again, safe and sound? I tell Grandfather this too, and he doesn't answer. I tell him that Mother never hugs us, and that in books it says that mothers look after their children when they're sick and there are songs that I know by heart about good mothers who stay up all night when their child has a fever. I sing him the songs twice, from start to finish.

In the morning I skip breakfast, and Grandfather spits out everything that Grandmother pushes into his mouth. I pretend to be asleep and listen to her sitting beside him on the bed and saying, "I wish you'd die already. I'm fed up. Die already. What did I do to deserve this? Why does God hate me so much?"

Later, when she carries him outside to the mattress, I sit next to him all day. I know it's still too early, but I keep looking up the street, waiting for my parents to arrive. I will recognize the bus.

My brothers talk about presents. My older brother wants them to bring him another remote-operated car that turns over, runs into walls, changes directions and keeps going. My younger brother wants the same thing but in a different color. They play video games all day, focusing on the screen. Around noon, Grandmother takes Grandfather inside because of the heat and shouts at me to come eat and then to lie down like my brothers, but I stay put.

In the afternoon she brings Grandfather back and he lies next to me. The closer we get to the time that I wrote down in my notebook, the more restless I am. Five o'clock comes and goes, and I know that something bad has happened. Now we only need to wait for the messenger. The sound of an unfamiliar car coming up our street is what scares me the most.

The bus is hardly late at all, fifteen minutes, maybe. My heart is pounding and I let loose a scream, "They're here." My brothers rush out toward the bus and so do I. My parents come down the steps. I calm down and give a big smile. They open the luggage compartment. Apart from the bags they took with them, I see they have some new ones. They divide the luggage among us and we carry everything home. My mother shakes her mother's hand and shouts to Grandfather as if he can only hear when you shout, "How are you, Father?"

PART SIX

A New Era

1

I sleep well for several hours, the longest stretch of sleep I've had all week. I only wake up toward evening. The whole family has gathered in my parents' living room. The front door is locked, despite the heat. Tonight we'll sleep here so that, if need be, we can all be together to defend whatever few food supplies we have left, and we'll also be closer to one another in case of any more shooting. The two little ones are asleep. A voice from outside takes my breath away for a second, and then I realize it's the muezzin calling people to evening prayers. Since the power was cut, his voice has been different. It's his own voice, not a prerecorded one. Finally the minaret is actually being used for its real purpose. For the first time in my life I hear a human voice, not a mechanized one, calling people to prayers, just like in the movies about the period of the prophet Muhammad.

My older brother decides to go to services in the mosque. "What for?" his wife asks. "You can pray here. That's a better idea. Who knows what could happen?" But my brother is adamant. "That's precisely why. Because of the 'who knows?' At least if anything does happen, I'll know I've fulfilled my duties to Allah."

My mother stands up and pleads with him, "Pray at home, for God's sake. Why leave the house now, in the dark?" But my brother turns a deaf ear to his wife and his mother. He takes his sandals and leaves. I lock the door behind him. My mother whispers a prayer for his safety, holding out her hands heavenward.

"Nothing will happen to him," my father says. "The mosque is practically next door. What could possibly happen?"

It's amazing how just a few days ago these were the noisiest hours in the village, the time when everyone would be outdoors. Loud music from cars and weddings was a permanent feature of our summer nights. Who could even hear the muezzin at such times? Nobody, despite the state-of-the-art loudspeakers on the minarets of the five mosques.

"I'm afraid he'll get arrested," my mother says.

"Don't be ridiculous. Who's going to arrest him? What's got into you?" Father tells her off.

"How can I tell?" she says. "They keep an eye on anyone who steps inside a mosque. Maybe they'll have a raid and take him too."

My older brother's wife grows increasingly agitated as she listens to this. "Of course," my father says. "Your son is Bin Laden. Stop this nonsense right now. Nobody's going to arrest anybody. He doesn't even have a beard. What's got into you? He'll be right back."

"Actually, he does look kind of suspicious. He hasn't had a shave in four days," my younger brother says with a chuckle.

I can still feel the wounds caused by this afternoon's stoning; the scenes with the neighbors and the children and the crowd outside our house linger on. I feel a strong need to avenge myself, a strange urge to restore my dignity, which I lost in a flash. But what can I do? If only I had a weapon. I wish I had a gun. I wish I were connected to one of the gangs. Then nobody would dare come near me or my family. But I'd never pull it off. I'd never even be admitted into one of those groups. I hate myself now for being unable to prove I'm strong, frightening, a man with pride.

My father turns on the radio again. There's a Head & Shoulders commercial in Arabic, followed by Chevrolet, Ship of the Desert. The newscast begins with coverage of the Egyptian president's state visit in the south of the republic and a cornerstone-laying ceremony for a few new food factories. Then they report on the president's wife's tour of a Cairo hospital for children with cancer. The Voice of Cairo reports that the president congratulated the Palestinians and the Israelis on their fervent efforts to put an end to the crisis and expressed his appreciation for the historic role of the U.S. president in this process. Next came the recorded voice of the president: "Both sides have had enough bloodshed. We are on the threshold of a new era, an era of peace and cooperation, an era that promises peace for our children. Never again will they know the suffering that our own generation has endured."

My younger brother laughs. Father says that on the day when the Voice of Cairo broadcasts the truth, we'll know that the East is about to become the strongest empire in the universe. My father spins the dial rapidly to the news in Hebrew. It's eight P.M. and there's a special broadcast, longer than usual. On Israel TV too they're talking about serious progress in the negotiations, and the Israeli and Palestinian prime ministers can be heard complimenting one another in English.

What's going on here damn it? Is this for real, the news we're listening to? My older brother, knowing how tense things are, knocks softly on the door and announces, "It's me," to keep from frightening us. His wife rushes to the door and locks it again behind him. He says there's nothing to be afraid of, there's nobody outside and we might as well open the door to let some air in. "Do you want to die of lack of oxygen?" he asks. But the door stays shut.

I move to the kitchen and light up a cigarette. My younger brother joins me, gesturing to me to pass the cigarette over to him. He studies Father, and once he sees him immersed in conversation, takes my cigarette and draws deeply. He coughs and hands the cigarette right back to me. Father turns in the direction of the kitchen and my younger brother chastises me: "You're going to choke us all to death with your smoking. Enough of your cigarettes!" He chuckles.

Even though things in the village have never been this bad, at least not since the war of 1948, news of the peace that's about to prevail helps us keep calm. At least we know that nothing on the scale of a world war is about to descend on us. Maybe everything that's been happening is actually nothing more than a tactic because of the efforts to arrive at a complete cessation of the tensions with the Palestinians. Maybe it's really intended to prevent the Palestinian organizations that don't believe in negotiating with the Israelis from undermining the progress of the peace process with some terrorist attack that could lead to a complete turnabout in the political position of the average Israeli. Maybe damn it, the Israeli side didn't actually intend for the power and the water to be disconnected and it's still just a stupid mistake. The power cut stops the water supply too, after all. All it takes, in fact, is one bulldozer or tank to hit the power line and this is what happens.

My mother is the first to go into my room. She lines up three mattresses on the floor. The children are using the double bed. She returns to the living room and announces that she's going to try to take a nap. My older brother's wife gets up too, says, "Good night," and joins my mother. "I'll go to sleep too," my wife says, but before heading for my parents' bedroom, she joins me in the kitchen and asks if I'm hungry yet. "No," I tell her. She looks at me now the way she hasn't looked at me in a long time. "Good night," she whispers, and I feel that if there weren't so many people around, she might even have given me a kiss. I feel the blood rush to my cheeks and my face becomes flushed. "Good night," I reply, and keep my eyes fixed on her until she reaches the bedroom.

My father and my older brother enter the children's room. My older brother stretches out in his boyhood bed, and my father uses mine. My younger brother quickly takes the opportunity to ask me for a cigarette and sits down next to me at the kitchen table. I reach out and fiddle with the saltshaker, an item that has never been replaced. My parents never bought a new saltshaker because there was never any need to. My mother always put a few grains of rice into it with the salt to soak up the moisture, so the salt didn't become lumpy.

"You know," my younger brother says, "normally I'd be out in the streets of Tel Aviv now with my friends. Whenever we finish an exam we go out drinking. We do the most drinking after exams," he whispers, and turns around to check if the coast is clear. He continues whispering, even though I myself can barely hear him. "Tel Aviv is an amazing city, I tell you. After exams, we don't just have beer the way we usually do. We go completely crazy. I'd waste four hundred shekels on booze right now if I could. I'd go for the pricey whiskey or Jägermeister. Do you like Jäger? It's great with lemon, you know. I don't really understand why you came back here. I don't understand you. I'd never come back. No way. I'd stay in Tel Aviv for the rest of my life, or run away to some country in Europe, or to Canada. The Canadians are easy with visas. I'd marry someone local and become a full citizen. Sure, they have their xenophobes and the anti-Muslims, but I'm telling you, from what my Christian friends tell me, the ones whose brothers emigrated there, what they call racism in London, say, is about the same as what we would call left-wing opinions here. It's a whole different world. The problem with London is that the pubs close at about eight P.M. I don't get it. If I want a night out on the town with some friends, we only get started at about eleven or twelve.

"Tell me," my brother asks, looking straight at me, "why are things like this? Do you ever ask yourself why we have to be this way? And the problem is that it isn't only us, it's all the Arabs. Why?" He takes another drag, rubs his eyes hard because of the smoke that gets into them and continues. "Sometimes when I see all those music festivals on Cairo TV, or Beirut or even Jordan, you know, I tell myself, isn't it great, how those people have festivals with the best Arab singers? You just buy a ticket and go to a performance. I've always dreamed of going to a concert in some Arab country or to celebrate Id el-Fitr in Damascus, say. Wouldn't that be great? The whole country celebrates it, like an official holiday. I mean, it's not like here, where they won't even give you a day off to celebrate your holidays. . . . But I find myself feeling sorry for those people, know what I mean? All those kids dancing at concerts or celebrating Ramadan. Every time I remember what kind of a regime they have, I feel sorry for them when I see them dance, and I don't understand why nothing changes in their situation. How could it be that all the Arab countries are like that?"

I look at him, and he smiles, giving off a kind of "Hmmmm." I continue playing with the saltshaker and don't say anything, though he's expecting a response. "I never think about those things," I tell him after a while.

"I'm not like that, I'm not like you," he says, squashing his cigarette in an ashtray and exhaling the last coil of smoke through his nostrils. "I don't feel like sleeping next to Father," he says. "I guess I'll take the sofa and you'll sleep on the bed, okay?" I nod and know I won't get any sleep tonight. "I'm not tired yet," I tell my brother.

"Neither am I. But I guess we ought to try and get some sleep, to make the time go by faster."

My brother lies down on the three-seater, which is barely large enough for him. He puts his head on one armrest and his feet on the other. The house is almost silent, except for an occasional cough or the sound of breathing.

I take off my shirt. It's filthy already, even though I just put it on a few hours ago. Ever since the closure began I haven't been able to shower but at least I've put on clean clothes, in the hope that they would offset the dirt. I reach for the back of my neck and scratch it gently. A thick layer of dirt gathers under my fingernails. I take a toothpick from the holder on the table in front of me and try to scrape away the dirt caked between my nails and fingers.

I don't want to stay here either. I'll leave as soon as I can. How can I possibly stay on here with neighbors who attacked me the way they did? How can I keep running into them? How can I go back into the grocery store after what the owner did to me today? How can I even feel safe in a place like this? I'm getting away from here, and that's final. I feel now that I can let my wife in on what I've been going through. When she spoke to me before going to lie down, I felt I could tell her everything, that I don't really have a job anymore. I felt she would have hugged me and comforted me. She would even have said something to make me feel better. I'm going to do it, to tell her everything, and we'll turn over a new leaf. I'm sure she'll understand what I'm going through. I'll find another job, and I'll go on moonlighting at the paper, in the hope that something better will turn up. There's no telling what's going to happen. But I'm going to find something else, anything. And who knows, maybe one of the places I sent my résumé has been trying to get in touch with me over these past few days, but can't. We'll live in a small apartment in a downscale neighborhood. We could even rent a one-room apartment for now, and put baby's crib next to us. We can live in a single room till she turns one. After that, we'll figure out something. By then I'll find something else, I'm sure of it, and things will get better and we'll be able to afford to move to something roomier. A two-room apartment with a small kitchen will do fine. We don't need a living room. Nobody comes to visit us anyway. A small kitchen with a table for three is plenty.

I've got to get out of here first chance I get. I'm sure my wife will be pleased. She hated the whole thing to begin with. She'll find another job. There's always a shortage of Arabic teachers, especially if we move to Tel Aviv or Jerusalem. She could work in Jaffa or in East Jerusalem. Very few of the Arab inhabitants in the mixed cities finish high school, so there are no local teachers, and there are always vacancies, and the outsiders are the ones who call the shots in the school system. Her best chance is in the Arab neighborhoods in Jewish cities. But we would not live in such a neighborhood, which seems as bad as here—worse, in fact. We'd do better living in a different neighborhood. In spite of everything, it's much safer living in a

Jewish neighborhood. The fact is that despite all the shit we had to put up with there, nobody ever attacked us, at least not physically. At least they have policemen and law enforcement. Now that I think of it, I lived there for more than ten years and I never—but never—heard a single shot.

2

uddenly a strong light fills the entire house. I hear myself yelling in fear—a short yell—then I bend over and cover my eyes. This light is very painful. My heart is pounding even though I realize now that it's simply the power that's come back on. The sudden brightness wakes my brother, who's been sleeping on the sofa facing me. "Yeah!" he says. "Is that it?" Almost all of the light switches in the house have been switched on. The light went on in my parents' bedroom too. The two children wake up and immediately start crying. My father emerges from the children's room, and my mother from hers and my father's bedroom, smiling broadly. She applauds softly, like a little girl who's just received a new toy. *"El-hamdulilah,"* she says. My wife and my older brother's wife stay in the bedroom with the children and try to calm them down, but I can hear how happy they are.

They're chuckling and their tone of voice is different. Everyone is smiling, and I hear how enormously relieved they are. I'm actually enjoying the noise that sounded so strong and surprising at first—the familiar droning of the refrigerator and the air conditioner and the incessant hum of the TV at my parents' house. My dad walks over to the air conditioner, puts his face up close and talks to it: "Welcome back, *ahalan u-sahalan.* How we missed you."

This is it, I tell myself, it's all over now. My mother tries to turn on the faucet in the kitchen sink. The water isn't flowing yet, but there's the sound of water pressure building up, the sound you always hear after it's been off for a while. My father says it's the sound of air and that we'll have water too pretty soon. It'll take time, but the sound proves that the water system is working. "It's a matter of a few hours, or even less," Father says, and lights a cigarette, then turns on the TV, where nothing has changed. It's almost two A.M. and there is nothing on Israel TV. On the Arab cable networks everything looks the same—Lebanese singers go on singing love songs, wiry dancers in alluring clothes sway seductively. The Saudi channels are teaching little children how to read the Koran, and the Egyptian channels are showing reruns of familiar series. My wife comes out with the baby, smiling, rocking her gently. You can tell she's happy. She looks at one of the series and says, "There's Nour el-Sharif, everything's okay." She and my older brother's wife are laughing.

I pick up the telephone receiver and hear a dial tone. I report this to everyone, reinforcing their collective sense of victory. I heave a sigh of relief. Tomorrow morning I'll try to phone the paper. Maybe they'll want me to do a write-up after all. Too bad it will only be for the following day. Tomorrow's paper closed at midnight. My father opens the locked door and goes out. We all follow. The entire village is lit up. Instead of turning off the extra lights, we join in the improvised "electricity party" that reassures us it's no illusion. It looks like the entire village has come alive. There are lights on in every house, and everybody's up, like just before a holiday. The familiar sounds of summer evenings are back. Sounds of happiness, of TV sets, of children playing and of parents trying to get them to settle down. Some of our neighbors are out on their balconies, smiling broadly. The neighbor who was assailing our house earlier today, spurred on by the crowd, is smiling at us now and yelling, "The electricity's working, the electricity's working," as if nothing has changed, as if she's forgotten what she did to us and what we did to her. Even the grocery store owner is shouting to us, laughing, overjoyed. "We can have a shower at last," my father says, and reminds us that we can remove the lump of gypsum from the sewage pipe. "I'll get it out," I say gleefully.

I go back inside. Everyone else is still outdoors. I look for the water bottle and gulp down almost all of it. The Egyptian singer is still singing love songs on TV. I look out the kitchen window in the direction of my house and my brother's. They are lit up too. I'll go over there.

My older brother joins me, and my younger brother decides to come along too. The rest of the family stays with my parents. It's best that way. The front door of my house is broken, but not too badly, and I can still lock it. I just need to replace one of the handles. There are lights on everywhere. The house itself is filthy. The doors to the kitchen cabinets are open wide and all of the shelves are bare. They didn't leave a thing in the refrigerator either. It's wide open, and there's a light on inside. My brothers and I close all the doors. There's nothing missing except food. In the storeroom I discover they took the olive oil too and all of the containers of olives. Never mind. The faucets give off the same sound of air pressure, and the occasional spurt.

"It's okay. Just a little dirt, that's all," my younger brother says, and asks for a pack of cigarettes and the lighter. I go upstairs. The bedroom is just the way it was before, as if my wife and I are getting up to another ordinary morning, another day of work. I turn off the bedroom light, then check the baby's room and take a look at all her toys. We'll go back to playing with her in here. I turn out that light too and walk up the stairs leading to the roof. First I bend a little to catch sight of the tanks to the north. I can hear them, but not as loudly as before. The sound of the return to normal in the village overrides the sound of the tanks which I kept hearing so loudly these past few nights. I look up slowly and see their headlights. They're moving, they're in motion, they're on their way out of here, leaving a trail of dust behind. Now I really know it's all over.

My younger brother follows me up. "They're leaving," I tell him. He smiles and looks in the direction of the tanks and the jeeps as they move away from the boundaries of the village. "What was it all about?" he asks.

"We'll know that tomorrow," I reply, and walk toward the water tank on the roof. "I suppose things will be much better now." I bend over and look inside. It's beginning to fill up with water. "I'm telling you, things will be much better than they were. You'll see." My younger brother waves at the family downstairs. "Everything okay?" he asks, and I can hear my older brother answer from below. "Sure, no big deal. They hardly took anything. How about you?"

"Same here," my younger brother answers. "I'm watching the military tanks. They're leaving. *Salamat.*" He says to me, "Give me another cigarette. Let's celebrate a little before I go back home."

3

It's almost four A.M. I go into the bathroom and stand completely still under the stream of water. I lower my head and
let the water land on my scalp and drip down over my whole
body. A brown puddle forms at my feet. Slowly the brownness
fades, but the layer of dirt clings fast to my body. I rub my head
with a generous dollop of shampoo. My hair has never felt this
way before—tangled and bristly. One rinse isn't enough to
soften it, and I squeeze out some more shampoo, working it
into my hair and across my scalp. But even though it's no longer
dirty, my hair refuses to go back to its former state. I wash my
face with soap. My wounds burn at the touch of the lather. I
ignore the burning sensation and try to be more gentle. I can't
shave my beard off yet. I have to wait for the sores to heal first.
It won't take long, maybe two or three days. I use a brush to
clean my hands, my stomach, my back and my legs. After every
part of my body that I clean, I rest a little, lift up my head and
let the water run down my face and over my closed eyes. I open
my mouth and let the water in.

I won't go to work tomorrow, but I can't wait till morning to pick up the phone to one of the editors and find out if

they're interested in a story. If they are, I'll write it from home and send it in by e-mail. Enough is enough, I'm not going to make a fool of myself anymore. I'm not going to go into the office just to sit around doing nothing, not after what I've been through this week, not with these sores. If I go in tomorrow, I'll look like a beggar.

From now on, I won't go in unless they ask me to, the bastards, and if they don't want this story from me, I guess it means they don't want to see me anymore at all. Normally the papers have a field day if a reporter of theirs experiences anything even remotely as incredible as what I've been through. Reporters who were involved in a car accident and emerged with a scratch have been given front-page coverage damn it, and headlines about what it's like: "Look Death in the Eye—Our Reporter Was Involved in a Traffic Accident and Miraculously Survived." If they don't want my story, I'll try to sell it to a different paper. I'll tell them so. Maybe it will scare them a little, but then again, maybe they won't give a damn. We'll see tomorrow. Only over the phone—I'm not going down there.

My wife comes into the bathroom and looks at me, smiling. "She's asleep," she whispers, and starts to undress. "How I've missed water," she says. "I'll go straight from the shower to school. I'm going to spend at least two hours in the shower."

I look at my wife and study her body. How pregnancy and childbirth have made it expand. I study her face and she looks bashful, delicate, still embarrassed as she stands before me naked. It's like that day, the first day I saw her. "You'll never find a wife like her," my mother said. "She comes from a very good family," my father pointed out, and after my parents spoke with hers and received their approval in principle, the three of us went to propose to her. We sat in the living room, the best-tended room in their house—a big, colorful room with black leather sofas surrounded by vases with plastic flowers. A painting of a waterfall and lots of green trees on either side of a lake adorned one of the walls. In the center of the table was a large bowl of fruit and next to it a big copper vessel for making coffee, standing there like a sculpture. She wasn't there waiting for us, and only arrived after her parents had welcomed us and we'd taken our places on the sofas. She was wearing a green dress that rustled like the plastic bags at the supermarket.

I look at her and recall the girl I saw on that visit, her body disappearing into her dress, her head lowered as she took my hand with her fingertips, so delicately that I could barely feel them. I felt uncomfortable at having planned the usual kind of handshake, using my full hand. I liked her handshake, actually, I'd never had anyone shake my hand that way before, gently, shyly. She really was good-looking. I'd never sat next to such a pretty girl, and I'd never dreamed I'd marry anyone like that. She looked like a high school student, though she had graduated two years earlier. Thin body, white face. Everything about her was a tad too small. She reminded me of the good girls in the Egyptian serials, which thrilled me.

I couldn't believe such girls really existed. Women who were actually little girls. I tried not to stare, and made do with quick, stolen glances. I knew I mustn't behave like an animal, but I also knew I wanted to marry her. After a few days of waiting, the time came for the official consent. Our next meeting added up to a handshake and an exchange of greetings after reading verses of the Koran as part of the engagement ceremony. When I took her hand in order to put on the ring that my mother had bought in her size, I felt my erection, and was terribly embarrassed. Never in my life had I held such delicate hands in mine and such thin white fingers. Two months later, we were married. Ten months later, our daughter was born.

"Make room for me," she says with a laugh, and her body touches mine under the water. She hugs me and I push her away. "I've got to rinse myself off again," I say, which she finds funny, even though I meant it seriously. I get out of the bath and wrap myself in a towel. "Where to?" she asks with an apologetic look in her eyes. "Stay here, I've missed you. How about you?"

"Me too," I say. "But I prefer the bed. I'll wait for you outside."

"Just don't fall asleep."

"I won't."

4

I get dressed, pull back the curtain of the second-floor bedroom window and look out over the village. Everyone is awake, and it looks like nobody intends to get any sleep tonight. It's as if the light and the water are about to disappear all at once and everyone wants to make the most of them for as long as possible. I hear a helicopter nearby, probably covering the soldiers on their way back to base. They'll be calling from the bank tomorrow. No, not tomorrow, it could take time, because the local branch burned down. I hope my overdraft disappears, I hope the last withdrawal, which was done manually, doesn't show up. There was no electricity, after all, and the one form that I signed probably went up in flames. This thought cheers me. I only hope my brother will go easy on me this time. I know him—if he remembers, he'll debit me again. I won't mention it to him. He can do whatever he wants, but I think it isn't fair to write off everyone else's debts and to keep track of mine. The last withdrawal won't change anything anyway. I've just dipped in a little bit deeper than I should, that's all. It'll be okay.

My wife is still in the shower. I'll go downstairs, meanwhile, to my study. On the bottom floor, I work my way between the smudges on the floor, trying not to get my feet dirty again. I turn on the computer. I'll check my e-mail. Ever since I stopped working, I've made a point of checking messages. I'm forever expecting the one that will let me know everything is about to change. When I'm not home, I check my voice mail every five minutes or so, and whenever I see an Internet connection, I log on to see if there's anything new. The truth is that when I'm home, I lift the receiver and check for the tone that signals an incoming message. Who knows—maybe I missed a call, maybe the phone was out of order. No new messages. I figure maybe it has something to do with the power cut and the fact that the phone lines were dead so that incoming messages couldn't be received. I know it isn't true, but still maybe, just maybe, there really was some special kind of glitch.

I won't manage to get any sleep anyway, till I can call the editor. Maybe at eight o'clock. Anything earlier would be overdoing it. Even eight is pretty early for an editor who doesn't put the paper to bed before midnight. I've got about four more hours to kill until then. I log in to one of the Hebrew news sites. There are dozens of them. People need to know what's happening every minute. Something can happen every five minutes and people don't have the patience to wait for the half-hourly newscast. Half an hour is too long in this fucking place. It takes the computer a long time to link up to Ynet. Too bad I don't have broadband. It takes forever for the home page to come up. While the computer calls up the visuals, all I can read is the headline. "Historic Peace Treaty Between Israel and the Palestinians," the banner headline announces. Very slowly, I can make out the picture, as it becomes less and less blurry. The Israeli prime minister and the Palestinian prime minister are shaking hands, with the U.S. president in the background.

Wow! A historic peace treaty! I discover myself smiling from ear to ear. I can't help it. That's it. It's all over. If our discomfort of the past few days spells peace between Palestinians and Israelis, I forgive everyone for everything. I know that peace with the Palestinians changes the whole picture and directly affects the attitude of the Jews and of Israeli Arabs. The Jews will start doing their shopping here in the village again, they'll be all over the place, people will smile more, we'll feel safer in the streets, on the buses, on the beach. It's all over. We're not going to have to feel suspicious, we'll go back to being almost-citizens. Everything will be different. I haven't forgotten how, right after the Oslo Accords, people used to say that it was time to improve the status of the Israeli Arabs. That's it, it's happening now. I remember how the media kept looking for Arab reporters who could serve as an example of the change that was under way. After the first peace treaty, we began seeing a few Arab moderators. The second Intifada wiped them out, but now things are getting back to normal. Things will be okay. Actually I too got my job at the paper after the first peace treaties and, to tell the truth, my fall from grace only happened after they collapsed because of this fucking Intifada. No more. Especially since peace also means a better economy. I'm sure those business and finance reporters will be celebrating tomorrow with the stock market investors, shares will go sky-high and the U.S. dollar will drop as the value of the shekel rises.

Finally there's a complete picture on the screen. Finally I can see the lawn under the feet of the smiling leaders, and the caption: "The three leaders after signing the permanent agreement." Who would have believed that the Israelis and the Palestinians would sign such an agreement? That's it, no more negotiations, crises, breaches and arguments about the status of Jerusalem, the return of the refugees and the dismantling of settlements. A permanent agreement is a permanent agreement.

The text reads: "Following intense deliberations, the final version of the peace agreement with the Palestinians was signed yesterday. Jerusalem will be divided, the Old City will come under UN supervision, Jews will have access to the Western Wall. Most of the settlements will be dismantled and will be repopulated with Palestinian refugees returning from the camps in Lebanon and Syria. The large blocks of settlements will be permanently annexed to the State of Israel. In return, the Palestinian Authority has received Israeli lands in direct proportion to the size of the settlements."

Wow! Unbelievable. On the face of it, this is a pretty major victory for the Palestinians. Israel could never have agreed to divide Jerusalem, to allow refugees to return and to dismantle most of the settlements. That's impossible. But it's a fact. There, another picture is coming up on the screen. This one's a map with a caption: "The State of Israel has clearly established borders at last." The Palestinians have received everything they asked for, almost the entire West Bank. According to the colored legend underneath the map, the Palestinians are in red and the Israelis are in green. The orange indicates blocks of settlements that will remain Israeli—very few of them, in fact—and they're pretty close to the Green Line—places like Ariel, Gilo, Pisgat Zeev. And the territories being handed over to the Palestinians are colored blue. Our village is colored blue. All of Wadi Ara and Triangle are blue. It must be a mistake. Some idiot graphic artist who always thought that Wadi Ara and the Triangle are both located on the West Bank.

5

The phone wakes me at six. I jump up, frightened. It takes a few seconds for me to calm down and realize it's just the phone. "Hello," I'm almost shouting, convinced there's been an accident. Early morning phone calls have always frightened me.

"Are you asleep?" Father asks. "Turn on the TV, Channel Two."

"What happened?"

"Just turn on the TV."

"Is something wrong?" my wife asks. She's sitting up in bed already.

"No," I tell her. "No, nothing's wrong. I guess they're filming the village for TV. I'm going down to watch. Go back to sleep."

It's six o'clock now. Before I turn on the TV, I check to see if there's water. The water is running. The Channel Two announcers are in the studio. The caption reads, "Special Broadcast," and below, down on the right, is the logo, "Peace has arrived." There are a few guests in the studio. No Arabs. Two of the senior announcers are sitting side by side. To the right is a large group of invited guests and to the left is our commentator on security affairs, Arabs, the economy. They're interviewing the chairman of the Settlers' Association.

"The association has issued unequivocal instructions to uphold the agreements. This is a heavy price for an agreement. We are giving up our homes. We spent years fighting for the right to those homes, and we shed precious blood in the process. I am convinced that most of the settlers of the West Bank and the Gaza Strip will abide by the agreement and that the evacuation will be reasonably smooth. I condemn in advance any unruly behavior by extremists. They in no way represent the community of settlers," the chairman says. He goes on to note that he is convinced the Palestinian Authority will not lose much time in breaking the agreements and that the government will then realize what a terrible mistake it made. Photos taken on the previous day or two appear in the background, with the dates underneath, showing the settlers loading up the trucks and leaving their homes.

The next person to be interviewed is a representative of the Israeli left. He sits there with a smile on his face. To tell the truth, they all seem pretty calm. "This is undoubtedly a historic step," says the speaker, who is furthest to the left among the Jewish Members of Knesset. "A historic step in which we have stopped controlling, occupying and repressing an entire nation. This is a decisive and vital step for the democracy of the State of Israel. We have been freed of the curse of occupation and created clear boundaries for our tiny country. I congratulate the prime minister on these bold steps. Our party will do whatever it can to ensure that this peace agreement receives the long-lasting support of the members of the opposition too." Then, the screen shows demonstrations of joy in the cities of the West Bank and Gaza. Lots of buses are unloading Palestinian prisoners, who are seen in the warm embrace of their loved ones. Veiled women are sprinkling candy on passersby, children are hoisting pictures of the Palestinian leader.

"At long last, the Zionist dream is coming true," one well-known Israeli professor is telling the moderators. The caption gives the professor's name and university affiliation, and in smaller print, "Demographer." "The greatest threat confronting the State of Israel is no longer," the professor explains. "The Jewish identity of the state has never been clearer. The wise step taken by the present government was overdue. Long overdue, in fact. According to the figures we have, in less than two years the Palestinians living between the Jordan River and the Mediterranean would have outnumbered the Jews. Now we can expect an overwhelming and permanent Jewish majority. In fact, the population of the State of Israel has now become almost one hundred percent Jewish. At long last, a truly Jewish state."

The next image is that of the new map of Israel. What's going on here damn it? I ask myself. The phone rings again. "Did you see that?" my father asks.

"Yes," I answer, but I don't know what he is referring to—the peace treaty that's just been signed, the evacuation of the settlements or the map that we're seeing on the screen. A list of the places that Israel has handed over to the Palestinian Authority appears on the screen in alphabetical order. Now I understand.

"What's going on? The SOBs. It just can't be," my father says. I don't answer. There's nothing to say. "Look, our village is on the list," Father says. I see it, I see it. The announcer can be heard reporting on the transfer of lands to the Palestinian Authority. Scenes from last night's events appear on the screen—the tanks pulling out of the Arab towns and villages. There, I can see Um-el Fahm now, and Taybeh and Nazareth. . . . "With few exceptions," the announcer says, "the transfer of authority to the Palestinians was relatively uneventful."

"Anything wrong?" my wife asks as she comes down the stairs.

"I think we're Palestinian now," I tell her. "We've been transferred to the Palestinian Authority."

"Does that mean we have school today?"

6

Oh my God, oh my God, oh my God. What do we do now? It's all over. My parents and my older brother are standing on the balcony, looking out over the street, over the village. Father's face is that of a man in mourning. Mother is holding her cheek with her left hand, and doesn't say a word. Only my younger brother is smiling and signaling to me, when nobody's looking, that he's dying for a cigarette. I don't dare to laugh, because you're not supposed to laugh when you're in mourning. My older brother says it's the will of Allah and he quotes a verse of the Koran to the effect that you should not hate anything because you do not know when it might turn out to be useful. "What do you mean, 'useful'?" Father says. "Sometimes you'd do better to keep quiet." This only broadens the smile on my younger brother's face. Father is lashing out at him too. "Keep quiet," he says. My brother clears his throat and tries to stifle his laughter.

A green jeep drives by, bearing the emblem of an eagle and a Palestinian flag. The neighbors follow it with their eyes. Nobody goes out into the streets, as if there were a curfew. "Long live Palestine. Long live Palestine." The slogan reverberates throughout the neighborhood, and everyone knows it's from Thurmus's tape recorder. Everyone knows the words. Thurmus is touting his wares with his cart, his music and his vat full of thurmus. "This is a holiday," he shouts. "Thurmus, *ya wallad*, salted thurmus." My younger brother thinks this is hysterically funny. "I didn't realize Thurmus was still alive," he says. Now everyone is smiling a little.

So what now? Nobody really knows. Is there school? Are we allowed out of the village? Just what do we do now? Very slowly, people begin venturing outside, some of them still not comprehending what has happened. They're chatting. "The Jews have sold us down the river," I hear the grocery store owner shout. From time to time we see a white jeep with a blue UN flag. It's the first time anyone from the UN has been through this village. They look at the inhabitants and wave at us, apparently assuming that we're supposed to be happy now just like people in cities on the West Bank.

Nobody really grasps the new reality yet. It seems like the overriding feeling is one of joy over the renewed electricity and water supply, and relief at the disappearance of the sense of imminent danger. The workers haven't cleared out the garbage today. A group of them can be seen marching up the road, near the mosque. Their laughter can be heard here too. Another jeep passes by, full of Palestinian policemen in blue uniforms. They stop next to the workers, who are cheering and applauding.

"Look at those *Daffawiyya* shitheads," one of the neighbors yells. His wife silences him at once, and it dawns on him that there is no point cursing this way under the new rulers.

My father has left the TV on, and I hear the special peace broadcast. It's a commercial break, advertising a new brand of Strauss ice cream. "The Israeli Arabs," I can hear someone say after the commercial, "never felt part of the State of Israel. They're really Palestinians, whose relatives live on the West Bank and in Gaza. The transfer of lands to the Palestinian Authority has spared Israel the enormous danger of a rising Islamic Movement and other nationalist movements from within. They should be pleased that we are enabling them to reunite. They've always complained about being discriminated against and about their minority status, and we should be pleased that our democracy will finally have real meaning. I hope the Palestinian population that was previously referred to as Israeli Arabs can serve as a bridge between the Arab world and Israel. They know us well, after all, they know Israeli society, our language and our democracy. They will play an important role in the democratic changes that will take place, if at all, in the Palestinian state."

"Democracy?" Father says. "If anyone dares to open his mouth now . . . they'll swallow us alive. To begin with, they've always said we sold ourselves to the Jews. But that's what all sorts of MKs and sheikhs wanted around here, right? Well, they got what they wanted, didn't they? Let's hear any of them say anything about his new government."

"It's better than the Jewish shit," my younger brother blurts out. He sounds militant.

My father looks at him, his eyes ablaze. "Shut up, you. You don't have a clue. And I don't know what even gives you the right to talk." My father is shouting now. He seems very tense. "Have you asked yourself what's going to happen to your studies? Where will you continue studying? Where will you work anyhow? Have you given it any thought? That's assuming your new state has courts to begin with."

"At least we won't have every dog thinking he's king," my younger brother says. "At least when the police come in and enforce the law, those heroes with their weapons will see what law and order is all about. Just wait till those big-shot delinquents get a taste of the security forces now. We'll see what happens to all their machismo."

"Shut up," Father tells him. "Shut your trap."

My younger brother shuts up.

"What about the banks?" my older brother asks.

They're saying on TV that about one hundred thousand Israeli Arabs living in Haifa, in Jaffa and in other mixed cities will remain in Israel, but with Palestinian papers, and they'll vote in the Palestinian Authority elections. They'll be like temporary residents, like foreign workers. There's talk of reparations too, and of how the new Palestinians will be received in the warm embrace of their mother state.

My mobile phone rings. It's my editor-in-chief. "Congratulations," he says. "Well, are you people happy now? You've got a state of your own. Just kidding. . . . Listen, I'd like you to write something for us."

"Okay, sure."

"Actually, I'd like you to be our man in Palestine. You've got excellent Hebrew, and we need someone to report back to us from there now."

270

"Okay."

"In any case, I'd like a story for tomorrow. Even a thousand words, about the transfer of authority. You know, until two hours ago there was a gag order, so today's papers have nothing. Feel free to tell it all, including maybe a few lines of your private take on this. Give it a personal touch, maybe in the lead-in, or else at the end."

"Uh-huh."

"I'll be in touch with you later. I'll let you know what happens at the meeting. I think it ought to work out. Listen, there might be a bit of a problem with the pay, because we're into drastic budget cuts, so it won't be the way it was before, but your cost of living is going to be much lower now anyway, isn't it?"